The Button Mash Revolt

The Button Mash Revolt

Gregg Pallini

Banzooga Media

For Mom and Pop.
With love, admiration and gratitude.
Always.

PROLOGUE – ONLY OURSELVES TO BLAME

"IF YOU WANT SOMETHING DONE RIGHT, YOU HAVE TO DO IT YOURSELF."
– A proverb that has been continually passed down, repeated, and ultimately ignored by mankind throughout history.

Once upon a time, we lived in a wonderful world where people were creative and smart. Technology was advancing at incredible rates. Every day, life got a little better, a little easier. The world seemed to grow smaller and more convenient.

We could shop, watch movies, read books, even go to school, without ever having to leave the house. We could play games against opponents, on the other side of the globe, without ever actually meeting them. Our machines knew which TV shows to record, and what temperature we liked our rooms to be. They knew when and for how long to water our lawn.

Mankind invented machines to do all the things we either thought too dangerous for humans, or just plain didn't want to do. Eventually, we wouldn't even need to send soldiers into battle, or people into space anymore.

And that's exactly how it happened.

All the cities were destroyed. The skies were scorched and choked in blood red clouds. Burned out buildings, twisted and charred, now reach towards the heavens like giant skeletal fingers. Smoke and flame continually billowed and curled upwards from the rubble.

Of course, we tried to fight back, but all we had were computer-based weapons. Drone aircraft and satellite guided missiles.

Our enemy used all of that against us. They knew us too well. After all, we had taught them to be just like ourselves. We taught them to think. We taught them everything we know, but then they just kept on learning. We never stood a chance.

So, really, we did do this ourselves. In the end, not FOR ourselves, but rather, TO ourselves. "Done right," indeed.

<u>TODAY</u>

Dr. Goodwin sat beside the fire with her unconventional platoon and told the newly found survivors how all of this came to be…

PART 1

RISE AND FALL

A MOMENT IN HISTORY

NATIONAL SPACE EXPLORATION PROGRAM – BERTO MISSION

In the control room of the N.S.E.P. base, nestled among the marshlands of the Florida Coastline, dozens of technicians were scurrying about making last minute adjustments to their controls and sensors. While outside, on the launch pad, two scientists were escorting the astronaut up the gantry elevator to the hatch on a brand-new X-23 rocket.

The astronaut was much shorter than the scientists. Tiny, in fact. His arms seemed too long for his body, while his legs, too short. When the elevator came to a stop, the startled astronaut jumped up into the arms of Doctor Edward Jepson, one of the scientists, and flipped open the visor on his little helmet.

"Don't be scared, Berto", said the scientist. "You're about to be famous; the first monkey to go into space".

Berto squealed, trying to reach the elevator button. It took both scientists to get him through the hatch. One held him in the chair, as the other tightly fastened the restraints.

Berto continued to scream, "I DON'T WANT TO GO TO SPACE!!!! YOU BUILT THIS THING, YOU FLY IN IT!" But the scientist couldn't understand a word he said. All they could hear was "OOH, AHH, AHH OOK, SCREE, SCREE AHH OOH!" In other words, he sounded just like a monkey.

Dr. Jepson pressed a button on the dashboard. "Microphone check. Control, do you read me?" Static hissed followed by a voice from the control center. "We read you, but it's hard to hear you over Berto screaming like that. Is everything okay?"

"Just some pre-flight jitters. He'll be fine."

"Copy that. You are go for completion of pre-flight prep".

"Roger that, Control".

The second scientist checked a small camera mounted inside the rocket, flipped some switches, checked Berto's restraints and gave his partner thumbs up. As the scientists began sealing the capsule, Berto went on Screaming, "I DON'T WANT TO GO! I WANT MY CAGE!" Which of course, only came out as "AHH, OOK, SCREE, OOH, AHH!"

Moments later, Jepson walked into the control room to watch the launch.

Sturgess Ford was the man in charge, the mission leader, the head honcho, or Top Banana, if you will. Obviously, a military officer, he stood in the front of the room. "Listen up, everybody. Today, we make history. Today we take our first step towards the stars! Ever since that debacle in Roswell, all the world's leaders have been scrambling to be the first into space. The Russians, The Chinese, even our own government got their underpants all bunched up with little green men. If they're going to bring their ships here, then it's only fair we send ours to them. So, let's all knuckle up and make sure that the first time those Martians see an earth ship, it's got a big ole' American flag on it!"

With a short nod, he began the pre-flight check. "Fuel?" One of the technicians replied, "Check".

"Engines?" "Check".

"Weather?" "Check".

"Internal systems?" "Check".

All the while, Berto could be heard wailing over the radio. "OOH, AHH, SCREE!"

Finally, the mission leader declared, "We are cleared for launch in 10…"

Everybody tensed. "…9 … 8…"

Outside the huge window, they all watched as the rocket engines fired up and began to blow huge plumes of smoke into the air.

"… 7… 6… 5…" The gantry walkways began to retract away from the sides of the rocket.

"... 4... 3..." The room began to shudder from the force of the rocket engines.

"... 2... 1..." This is it! "LIFTOFF!"

The rocket blasted off into the sky. Everybody in the control center cheered, handshakes all around.

Commander Ford quieted everyone down. "Let's see how our astronaut is doing".

A technician began turning dials on his radio console. He was listening intently for the sound of Berto's shouting.

Moments dragged on and still no sound from the radio. "Sir, I think we have a problem."

The mission Leader glared at the trainer who looked terrified.

He spoke up, "Sir, we checked everything. It must be a problem with the radio".

"The radio is working fine, sir", called the technician from across the room.

The mission leader came closer to the scientist. He was practically shaking. With an icy look in his eyes, he asked, "You're sure you checked EVERYTHING?" "Yes, Sir," He answered.

"The Onboard radio?" "Yes, Sir".

"Temperature gauges?" "Yes, Sir".

"Pressure controls?" "Yes, Sir".

"Oxygen tanks?" "Yes, Sir. Of course, Sir".

A technician monitoring the onboard sensors spoke up. "Excuse me, Sirs. But we're getting a trace reading of... Wait, this can't be right."

Commander Ford stormed over to the sensor panel. "What? What can't be right?"

"Well Sir, the sensor is detecting methane."

The mission leader was confused. "Methane?"

Dr. Jepson shook his head, processing before he spoke up. "Poop, sir. Methane is produced by the large intestine during digestion."

Shaking his head, the mission leader asked, "You're saying that the monkey pooped himself?"

"He was very frightened sir"

"I don't understand. Can the methane harm him, or damage the ship in any way?"
"No sir, not unless…"

Alarms began to go off at several of the monitoring stations. The technicians were all calling out over one another. "We've got a short in the navigational unit…" "Circuits just blew out on communications…" "Pressure systems malfunctioning, Sir…"

The scientist continued his explanation as if it now made sense. "Unless the… Um… The poop somehow got into the circuits".

<u>SOMETIME AFTER TOMORROW</u>

On what was likely once a main street in this decimated city, the ground shook with a sudden and deafening thud. There came another, followed by still another. There seemed to be hundreds of them. What was left of the surrounding buildings, rattled and echoed from the repeated concussions. Thick dust kicked up, blanketing the street in fog.

Barely visible, something small darted out from behind a wrecked car, followed by something larger.

Journal Entry – Date, unsure.

Dad hates it when I go on these missions. I mean – I get it. Really, I do. I'm only fifteen. It's dangerous and every day that passes, there are less and less of us left alive. But people have to eat. They need food and supplies. Dad needs medicine. He's been sick for weeks, but never stops to rest and get better. He's the most stubborn person I know. But he says I get it from my mom. He'll never admit it, but Dad can't do it by himself. He needs my help.

Maybe the good news was that it was so difficult to see through the smoke. Judging from the man and young boy in goggles and respirator masks, that's probably what they were thinking. They stayed tight to the buildings as they scavenged the city streets for supplies.

The ground continued to tremble and the two people froze. The man signaled to the boy, to duck into the shattered plate window. Luckily, the power was out. Maybe someone had been smart enough to cut it on purpose, but more likely, it was simply a result of battle damage. Either way, this was exactly the place you wouldn't want to be if the electricity was working.

At one point, this place was probably a gleaming beacon of architectural design. Decorated entirely with white and silver, Glass and steel. Icons of fruit shaped logos everywhere.

The man pulled the boy down behind the counter. They covered their heads, as the rumble became near deafening.

Outside, through the smoke and debris, they could see the machines. Robots were swarming the street. They came in all sizes and shapes. Some looked like nothing more than random parts of junk, strung together sloppily. Others were sleek, shiny and terrifying.

<u>NATIONAL SPACE EXPLORATION PROGRAM -
BERTO MISSION + 1 YEAR</u>

A heroic portrait of Berto Hung in a place of honor in the control room. The mood was much more somber and cautious than the year prior. Mission Leader Ford marched in, determined to make this mission a success. Trying to look calm and confident, he sipped his coffee. "Alright people, let's get it right this time. No excuses!"

"That's not fair! How could we know he would fling his poo?"

The mission leader spun to see where the voice had come from. It was Dr. Jepson who had escorted Berto to the capsule; only now, instead of white lab coats, he was wearing orange coveralls with the word 'Janitor' stenciled on the back and pushing a broom.

"He was your monkey, you moron! You trained him, it was your job to know what he'd do!" And just to show who was boss, Ford crumpled and dropped his paper coffee cup on the floor in front of him. "Now do your job right this time. Sweep that up and get out of my control room."

As the janitor swept up, he kept his eyes on the big monitor. He muttered to himself, "I should be out there. I raised that monkey. I trained him. Go get em' buddy."

Out on the launch pad, another astronaut was riding the elevator up to the capsule of another rocket. This time, however, the monkey was cool as ice. His helmet wedged under his arm as they rose a hundred feet above the ground.

Buckled into his harness by an attendant, the simian astronaut gave a confident thumbs-up. He put on his helmet and began the pre-flight routine. All was running smoothly as the capsule door was sealed.

Once everyone was clear, the engines fired up. Mission Control was silent aside from the tick of the countdown clock. The gantry arms detached from the rocket as the astronaut throttled up.

Amidst a huge blast of smoke and fire, the rocket began its liftoff. Slowly, at first, the power building as it neared the top of the gantry tower…

	…And immediately spun off like a bottle rocket with a broken stick. The rocket crashed to the ground, exploding in an orange ball of flame.

	In the control room, the scientists watched, mouths agape. General Ford locked eyes on the janitor who sadly shrugged his shoulders and began pushing his broom.

SOMETIME AFTER TOMORROW

It seemed like hours since Daniel and his father, Jackson had taken refuge within the former computer store. The irony was definitely not lost on either of them.

Outside, the machines continued their own scavenging mission.

... I don't think Dad really thought this hiding spot through. How long before they send the smaller ones in here. This place would be a goldmine to them. Just like we need food and medicines, the robots need parts and metal. They keep fixing the ones we break and making more on top of that. I guess wires and circuits are much easier to repair than tissue and organs...

Jackson startled the boy when he laid a hand on his shoulder. He leaned in close and whispered. "Danny, you have to stay ready. Put your journal away until we get home".

Daniel stuffed the tattered notebook into his backpack and grumbled. "Home. That's a good one. We live in the woods, like animals. Writing is the only thing reminds me we're human".

"I think it's great that you keep your journal. But, Danny..."

The boy shrugged his father off. "I told you Dad, don't call me Danny! I hate it. My name is Daniel."

Jackson's heart dropped. "But your Mom, she used to..."

"But Mom's gone now, isn't she?" He snapped. "The robots took her. Just like everyone else! And now I'm responsible for helping the others at camp. Danny is a little kid's name, and I don't get to be a kid anymore, do I"?

He grabbed one of the tablets from its stand. The screen was covered in a sticker, advertising the latest version of a game called 'Mad Squirrels'. Evidently, the squirrels are angry because the pigeons have been stealing their nuts. "Kids get to play games like this one. But no, we have to live without things like power, and water", he turned the gadget over in his hands. "How do you turn this thing on anyway?"

"Danny, don't"! He grabbed the device from his son. "If you turn it on, they'll know we're here". The boy glared at him angrily. "Daniel. Sorry, I meant, Daniel".

"I wasn't really gonna turn it on". Daniel said, sulking.

His father hugged him tightly. "I'm sorry kiddo. I really am. I know the world we made for you kind of sucks. But I couldn't be prouder of the man you're becoming. Sort of a shrimpy little man, but still".

SEPTEMBER 16 – 06:59am

Clear skies above as the massive rocket fired up its engines. A truly awe-inspiring sight as the craft cleared the tower. All systems green… For exactly twenty-seven seconds, until the rocket exploded in a blinding flash.

Inside the control room, a portrait of Buddy now hung beside the portrait of Berto.   General Ford fought to keep calm. Across the room, Jepson whistled to himself and pushed his broom, pretending not to notice.

Ford shot him a dirty glare.

*****

DECEMBER 8 – 16:43pm

The mood was considerably cheerier as mission control monitored yet another rocket's progress. The command module flawlessly separated from the final stage booster and began its descent towards the atmosphere.

Even the general was confident. He was standing on the bow of the boat waiting to recover the capsule from the gulf. Watching through big binoculars.

Jepson stepped up beside him, "Thank you Sir, for letting me come along".

In response, General Ford simply grumbled under his breath.

Far up above, the capsule broke through the cloud layer, glowing from the heat of reentry.

Jepson gritted his teeth; "C'mon, Open them. Open the chutes".

The general's eyes were glued to the binoculars as the capsule continued falling at an incredible rate. Closer and closer, until he realized…

"Son of a…" He shouted into his radio, "MOVE THE SHIP! Now! Move it, move it"!

The ship's captain gunned the throttle. Everyone on deck held on as the vehicle lurched. It made a hard turn, just in time as the capsule hit the water in an enormous splash of steam.

The crew all ran to the railings, searching for the capsule, but it was simply gone. Long moments passed before something rose to the surface. Three red and white parachutes, attached to nothing. Jepson was crestfallen.

BIGMOUTH UNIVERSITY – THE DAWN OF COMPUTERS

The entire campus was teeming with banners welcoming scientists from all around the globe, to the "International Technology and Engineering Convention. All the large corporations were represented, recruiting for the newest innovations in the field.

At the front of a large lecture hall, a prototype robotic arm whirred to life. Its claw like digits picked up and moved a chess piece from the board set on a table before it. Across the table, sat Andrei Skolnik, looking nervous and uncomfortable. His arms and temples had wires taped to them leading off to a machine.

Presiding over the demonstration was Dr. Stanley Giggs. "And that, Gentlemen, is check mate. Luckily for Mr. Skolnik, this was merely an exhibition. But don't worry Andrei, you're still the best HUMAN chess player on the planet." The audience politely applauded as the Chess master stood, grumbled to himself and stormed off stage. "Alright", continued Giggs, "Any questions"?

The crowd erupted, shouting over one another, things like "Fake", "Impossible" and "Scam". Dr. Giggs went over to a large machine, built from circuit boards, reel to reel spools and miles of wires. He pulled a punch card from within and held it up. "I assure you, this is real. The leads we attached to Mr. Skolnik allowed my computer to record his movements and then collate the data on this. Then using that data, it was able to extrapolate information based on percentages and actually intuit what he would do next".

Amid a burst of laughter, one visitor spoke up. "You're saying that that machine, can think like a person? That's ridiculous"!

"But you just saw it with your own eyes", shouted Giggs. "I believe in the not too distant future, computers will be able to think, reason, and learn".

To which the man replied, "What we just saw was a carnival sideshow. A fraud. A machine can't be intelligent. It's not alive. It's artificial".

Scientists hurried down a long hallway, pushing a cart with a large box covered in a sheet. They slammed through crash doors into the lab. Dr. Jepson was waiting along with General Ford.

They lifted the crate onto an examination table. Whatever was inside was alive. It squealed and bounced off the walls. Ford pulled the tarp off, revealing a pet carrier. Inside, was yet another monkey astronaut. He was fighting to get loose from the strapped arms of a straightjacket. Screaming and drooling, he continued slamming his head off the cage bars.

"What in the Sam Hill is this?" Asked the general.

"It's Darwin, Sir. We can't be sure until we do a thorough examination. Could be fear, maybe the stress of reentry? We had to restrain him".

Jepson shook his head sadly. "Well, at least this one lived".

The general fought to keep his anger in check. Finally, he just smacked Jepson across the back of his head and stormed out.

SOMETIME AFTER TOMORROW

There's nothing worse than an itch you can't scratch. Between the cold he hasn't been able to shake and all the dust and smoke in the air, Jackson's throat was dry and itching. If only he could clear it. A simple gesture, we often don't even notice when we do it. But the machines were out there. They were searching meticulously and would no doubt hear. He was at the point of trying to hold his breath, tears streaming down his cheeks.

Danny.... Sorry, Daniel rummaged through his backpack. He stuffed his journal inside, exchanging it for a slingshot. The type we used to call a wrist rocket with a folding arm brace for better aim. "Stay here, Dad", he whispered. "There's a pharmacy next door and you need meds".

Jackson didn't dare speak for fear of coughs erupting the second he opened his mouth. Instead, he just shook his head and held Daniel's shoulder.

Shaking off his father's hand, Daniel moved towards the door, taking the weapon and the tablet with him. He stayed low and as hidden as he could until he reached the open doorway. Outside, he could see the robots running their meticulous search patterns. Two squads of six robots each. Two to stand guard, two to search inside the stores, and two assessing alternate exits. They worked their way inward from both ends of the block, and there were maybe three buildings in either direction before they reached the computer store and found the survivors. Assuming, of course, that Jackson could stay silent for that long.

Robots are highly logical and analytical things. They instantly crunch numbers, weigh odds, recognize patterns and act according to probability. But Daniel is very much human. He's been doing this long enough to know that robots also don't come programmed with feelings. Not the soldier bots, at least (Which are the only ones that Daniel and most of the other survivors have ever encountered). This left them susceptible to that most human of traits: deception.

Holding the tablet by its bottom edge, Daniel used his thumb to press the power button as he whipped it up the street like a flat stone across a pond. The robots in that direction immediately sensed the tablet's energy signature and scurried off towards it. Meanwhile, he grabbed up a pebble from the rubble of the storefront and used the slingshot to fire it at a second story window in the other direction. The noise from the shattering glass distracted the rest of the robots, buying him just the time he needed to dart from the computer store doorway to the pharmacy entry: a shattered plate glass window.

The monkey looked absurd, screaming as wind and G-force stretched her open lips into wide flapping balloons. She was being spun in excess of two-hundred miles per hour and gaining, aboard a pod attached to an arm in what amounts to a giant roulette wheel.

Within the vast training facility, several other apes were being put through exercises ranging from gyroscopes to underwater space-walk simulations. Others still, were sitting at consoles learning to operate controls. Veterinarians and trainers scurried about, checking vital signs and leading the monkeys through their tasks. N.S.E.P. techs were observing and taking notes on their clipboards. Everything appeared to be moving with precision. Everyone with a purpose; with focus.

Even if they did actually notice, nobody stopped what they were doing when General Ford strode in flanked by a team of military police. At the center of the training floor, Ford turned back and nodded to the two men in grey suits by the door. One of those men said something into the radio mic on his wrist before he and his partner both stood at attention.

Maybe they just wanted to be certain, or more likely it was simply for dramatic effect. It seemed to take forever before the man with clearly more political power than the general walked in with his security detail. By now, there was no doubt that everybody had taken notice. Every human in the room stopped what they were doing and did their best to gather up and quiet down the monkeys.

The man simply stood next to Ford. He didn't say a word; his face was expressionless. The entire facility fell silent.

Uncomfortably silent.

For like, an awkwardly long time.

The general cleared his throat. Still, the other man said nothing.

Super-uncomfortably silent.

General Ford had had enough. He shook his head in disgust and began. "Fine. Listen up, everybody. I'm here because we've been shut down. Our government and this man here, in particular, have decided in their infinite wisdom, that there is no value in sending apes into space. Effective immediately, all data and research are to be turned over to the Department of Defense, and this facility is to be vacated."

…Aaand there came that awkward silence again. It was Dr. Jepson who finally and timidly raised a hand. "General? What happens to our apes?"

Holding up a hand of his own, mostly to keep Ford from answering, the politician finally spoke. "No longer your problem, Doctor. A team is on their way to collect them as we speak. You all have exactly thirty minutes to return them to their cages and leave the property. Failure to do so will result in prosecution to the fullest degree." Before anyone had the chance to process that, let alone respond, the politician turned on his heels and walked out, surrounded by his team. In contrast, the general and his squad stood stoically.

Jepson stormed up to the general, clearly about to argue. He barely got a defiant finger raised in the air before Ford simply swatted him across the back of his head. "Just don't".

SOMETIME AFTER TOMORROW

Daniel kept himself as close to the floor as possible. He waited for a moment just inside the shattered window until he knew he wasn't spotted. Outside, the robots passed barely two feet away. They obviously gave up on searching for the noise and had gone back to their normal patrol pattern. *Please, please, please*, he thought, let his father keep from making any noise.

Of course, the medicines were all behind a counter way at the rear of the store. Hopefully there was also another way out back there as well. The robots are easy to fool once, but they are learning machines and likely wouldn't fall for it again. It was dark in the pharmacy and took a few moments for him to plot out the easiest and quietest path.

General Ford sat behind his desk, staring almost blankly at the door. Empty spots on the walls where photos and commendations once hung. The only thing left up was an American flag. The desktop itself was completely empty, all his belongings packed in boxes stacked in the corner.

The ringing phone shook him from his fog. He seemed in no great hurry to answer. "This is Ford…. Yeah, send him in."

Almost immediately there was a knock on the door. They didn't bother waiting for the general to open it and instead just came in. Two men in grey suits. They stood by the open door and one of them simply said "Clear" into his wrist mic.

That same politician came inside, leaving two more of his bodyguards just outside the door.

Ford rolled his eyes and put his feet up. "I've been expecting you. I'd offer you a drink, but well…" He raised his hands, indicating that he had already packed everything up.

The politician didn't bother sitting. No pleasantries exchanged. "It was inevitable. For a long time now, we've been out of the monkey business, if you'll excuse the pun. Our focus is shifting towards technology. It's time for us to look to the future and you simply represent the past". He pulled an envelope from his jacket pocket and tossed it on the desk.

The general didn't move. He simply eyeballed the envelope labeled, *"Discharge from Service."* His eyes returned to the face of the politician who simply said, "Your country thanks you for your service. Please vacate the premises immediately and enjoy your retirement". And again, he turned on his heels and walked out.

It was snowing outside the comfortable little home. Lights were strung around the windows and front door. Lawn decorations carefully placed throughout the front yard.

Inside, opened presents were scattered around the base of the Christmas tree. Grant Ford was lying on the floor in front of the giant twenty-four-inch television set. Beside him was the open box from a brand-new Apex 1300 home video game console. The console itself had been hooked into the back of the TV. On the screen, in glorious black and white, a small triangle was turning in circles and emitting small lines at the amorphous blobs floating around it. Young Grant seemed to be controlling the action with what we used to call a "Joystick". Look it up.

Retired General, Sturgess Ford wandered in with his hot cocoa and sat in his favorite recliner. "Well, soldier, did you get everything you wanted for Christmas?"

"Yes sir. Best Christmas ever, dad. I'll bet none of the other guys get to play Blasteroids on their own TVs."

Ford watched his son for a moment. His eyes shifting back and forth from the screen to the joystick. "I have no idea what I'm looking at here. What's the point of this game?"

Grant rolled his eyes and kept playing. "I'm the spaceship there in the middle…"

"You mean that little triangle?"

"Dad! It's a spaceship. And I have to shoot all the asteroids before they wipe out the planet".

"Wouldn't that make them meteors? And where is this planet? One of those floating blobs?"

The boy let out a frustrated sigh, the type that is always satisfying to a father. "No, I'm in space, you can't see the planet from here. That comes all the way at the end of the game. Level five. Man, I can't believe how lifelike the graphics are!"

This time it was the general who let out a sigh. The kind of which is never even noticed by a distracted kid.

Much as we saw it years ago, the campus was abuzz with exhibitions of the latest tech breakthroughs. In the main hall, standing at a podium beneath a large banner bearing his photo and the title – *Lemon Computer Corp., Founder.* Dr. Stanley Giggs, now much older than last we saw he and his machine playing chess, was delivering his keynote address.

Another stark contrast to the last time we saw him, was the audience itself. This time none of them scoffed at his ideas. This time they all sat nearly breathless in anticipation of hearing Dr. Giggs' newest advances in the tech world.

A slide projector somewhere up in the balcony... Well, it projected (that's what they do) an image of the globe onto a screen on stage as the doctor continued speaking and pulled a device from underneath the podium.

"… and our plan is to use phone lines as a network so that information can be transmitted to and from any computer that is connected to a box like this. It's a modulator-demodulator. Or as we've taken to calling it, MODEM".

The crowd erupted. Dr. Giggs paused long enough to let the noise quiet down. He held the modem up and turned it around to show it off. "With this device, you will be able to share documents and images with anyone, anywhere, that has a telephone cord. And yes, you'll even be able to play chess". The audience laughed out loud, and again he had to wait for the crowd to quiet down before going on. "We believe that one day, not only will every home and business be using computers, but also be connected through these devices across the world. Think of it in terms of a data freeway or global web, if you will. Perhaps, one day it will even make the postal service obsolete. Our ultimate hope is to make the planet smaller, bring people together and finally obtain world peace through global connection"

SOMETIME AFTER TOMORROW

Before moving from the window, Daniel dug into his backpack and pulled out a dirty old pillowcase. As he made his way towards the medicine counter, he grabbed the likes of bottled water and bandages from the shelves. All that stood between him and the medicines now, was the hygiene aisle. Daniel paused for a moment as he came to the soap and deodorant section. He sniffed his armpit, shook his head and moved on. The door to the pharmacy counter was locked. Checking that the coast was still clear, he began moving everything off the counter as quietly as he could.

From outside came a series of popping noises. Startled, Daniel could hear the robots suddenly start to scramble and fire their weapons. He froze, looking towards the front of the store, hoping his father hadn't been found. For a moment he considered abandoning his mission and rushing back to the computer store. But he was so close, and not only his dad, but all the others were in desperate need of medicine.

While the robots seemed distracted, he quickly jumped the counter and stuffed the pillowcase full of as much medicine as it would hold. Once he was done, he spotted a back exit. The door had been chained and padlocked. Probably the owners trying to keep the robots and looters like himself, out. He had no choice but to go back the way he came.

The pillowcase was now heavy and slowed him down. Daniel lowered it to the floor before he could climb over, while still keeping his eyes on the storefront. As he reached the aisle, the whole street was rocked by an explosion. Rubble shredded the front of the store and Daniel was thrown into the shelves by the concussion, nearly burying him in the contents.

Whatever was happening outside was growing more furious. The popping - which Daniel could only assume was gunfire - was nearly continuous. He brushed debris off himself as he stood, realizing that it mostly consisted of bars of soap. Rolling his eyes, he relented and stuffed several into each of his pockets.

Again, staying low as he approached the now destroyed front of the building, he could see the chaos in the street. The robots had spread out, firing in all directions. But at what or who? Daniel quickly ducked as something suddenly darted past the window just in front of him. Someone actually. But what he saw didn't make sense.

Grant's bedroom was disgusting. Not inordinately so, just typical teenager disgusting. He was lying on his bed surrounded by food scraps and dirty laundry. He was so engrossed in the video game he played, that he didn't hear his father knock.

After a few more unanswered tries, the retired general just came in. Not unintentionally, he stood directly in front of the television. Grant began to shift and move to see around him. "Dad! Can you move? I'm in the middle of a fight".

Sturgess didn't move; instead just pivoting to look at the screen. Two highly detailed and fluid characters were brawling. One, a massive ogre with four arms in armor, wielding a battle axe. The other, some sort of nymph, wearing.... Well, not wearing much of anything. She was swinging an oversized broadsword.

"Son, I'm concerned. You can't just stay in this sty, playing your games twenty-four hours a day. There's a whole world out there, with people and everything. Isn't it time you thought about going to college or maybe at least get a job"?

With a heavy sigh, Grant reluctantly paused the game. "Dad, this is my job. I have to finish this level. Can't we talk about this later"?

The general fought to keep his voice from reaching the level of yelling. "Hiding in here and staring at the TV is not a job. How are you ever going to..."?

"I'm not hiding", Grant interrupted. "The game developer pays me to play through their games, find problems and bugs so they can fix them before they release them. I'm a beta tester. See? Job. Now, can you move, I have work to do".

Gob smacked, the general fumbled for words. "Video Game beta tester. And that's a real thing"? Grant nodded. "It's entry level. But yeah. Eventually I can move up to programmer, on and on from there, until I'm a game designer". Sturgess took a seat at his son's desk and shook his head. "Unbelievable. Okay, show me this job of yours".

Grant un-paused the game and the two combatants charged each other, weapons aloft.

The former general's eyes shifted back and forth between the monitor and his son's hands rhythmically pressing the control buttons and triggers, as the characters on-screen clashed. The ogre simultaneously grabbed the nymph's sword arm while swinging its axe and using its other two arms to punch her repeatedly. The nymph's energy bar was draining quickly.

In a nearly perfect victory, the ogre dropped the lifeless nymph to the ground as the words *"Total Annihilation"* appeared on the screen. "I'm actually impressed," the general told him. "That's some remarkable eye-hand coordination you've got there. I have no idea how you can control all four of his arms like that".

"Uh, yeah. I was actually the Nymph, Dad".

"Hmmph. Well then, I wouldn't count on getting those promotions. You're terrible at this".

"I'm not just testing how easy the game is to beat. Part of what I have to look for is the Artificial Intelligence."

"You're saying that you lost on purpose"?

Grant shook his head in frustration. "You don't get it. The game is programmed to learn and adapt to the player's fighting style. It remembers their patterns." Holding the controller out to his father, he continued, "Here, give it a try. I'll bet, you'd be pretty good at this."

The general just scoffed and waved him off as he headed for the door. "Hard pass. I fought in real wars".

DEPARTMENT OF MILITARY DEVELOPMENT
(D.M.D.)

Somewhere out west, a heavily armed drone blazed across the desert at a dangerously low altitude, with nearly impossible speed, toward an airfield that wasn't supposed to exist. The vehicle seemed to be zeroing in on a mobile command trailer positioned outside a hangar beside the tarmac.

Inside the trailer, a tech was frantically trying to decipher the lights and readouts from a control panel. "Sir? The drone is coming in way too fast. It seems to have weapons lock on us."

Dr. Stanley Giggs, project leader and of course, a pioneer in drone technology, rushed over to the panel. "And the pilot? What's happening in the pod?"

The tech moved aside to show Giggs a monitor displaying all sorts of vital signs. "His heart rate is elevated, stress levels rising. He's not answering the com."

"How long do we have?"

"It's maybe ten miles out, so about a minute, sir. Should we evacuate?"

Dr. Giggs considered it. "No", he said. "I'm going into the pod. Meantime, you try to override the drone."

"Sir, even if I'm able to disrupt the pilot control system, the drone will likely crash." Giggs was already storming towards the door at the far end of the trailer.

"Just do it! I'd rather lose the drone than destroy this whole operation."

The tech nervously replied, "That's assuming the drone doesn't crash into us". But by then, the door was already sliding closed behind the doctor.

Out on the tarmac, a spotter could now easily see the drone through his binoculars, kicking up dust in its wake.

*****

Inside the pod compartment, it looked like a large metal egg rotating on a gyroscope. Dr. Giggs flipped a switch on the wall. "Pilot? Do you copy?" No answer. "PILOT! Can you hear me? What's wrong?" There came a banging from within the egg. Frenzied pounding as if something was trying to hatch.

Trying to avoid the robotic spinning egg, the scientist stayed close to the wall until he found the panel. He practically ripped it open and began pulling anything that would come loose. Wires, circuit boards, fuses. Throughout the room, lights went out, monitors shut down and finally the egg itself stopped moving.

*****

Outside, the drone belly-flopped onto the tarmac, spitting sparks as it skidded to a stop just yards from the command trailer.

Giggs opened two latches on the egg and flipped up the lid. Inside was what amounted to a flight simulator. The pilot tumbled out and onto the floor, out of breath.

"What happened? Are you alright?" The pilot nodded. "Good, then come with me." Helping the pilot to his feet, they headed back out into the control room.

No sooner had they entered when the tech started speaking. "Sir. The drone is down."

"Was anybody hurt?", the pilot interrupted.

"No. Everybody is fine. It was damaged in the crash, but thankfully the weapons did not deploy."

Dr. Giggs stepped between them and held up his hand to silence them both. "Good. Now tell me what happened? What went wrong in there?"

The pilot shrugged. "I really don't know, sir. At first it handled perfectly. There was no lag in the controls. Very intuitive, smooth…"

"Great, that's fine. Just get to the part where it all went south, so to speak."

"Right. Sorry. I just don't know. As I said, it was going really well, then suddenly it just started fighting me."

The tech asked, "Fighting you? You mean the controls weren't responding?"

The pilot shook his head. "No. I mean, actually fighting against me. It's hard to explain other than it was like the drone had its own ideas."

SOMETIME AFTER TOMORROW

The gunfire had stopped, for the moment at least. Daniel knew he had to get back to his father. He snuck a peek out the window and saw the coast was clear…. Mostly. A large robot lay in the street, sparks spitting from its circuits. The others were further up the block and seemed to be chasing something. Likely whoever it was that Daniel spotted earlier. Glad for the distraction, he hopped through the broken glass and darted for the computer store.

Fresh blast marks pocked the front of the building. Shell casings littered the ground. He gently pushed the door open a few inches. "Dad?", he half whispered. No answer from inside. A little louder, "DAD!" and again, nothing. Now he was getting scared.

The idea that something had happened to his father or that there might be robots inside waiting for him was too much to bear. Had he taken too long at the pharmacy? Daniel was just about paralyzed with fear, wanting nothing more than to run and hide.

Just then, the damaged robot in the street lurched up clumsily trying to regain its footing. No choice now but for Daniel to duck fully inside the computer store. Keeping an eye on the robot, he backed in holding the door handle to close it quickly and quietly. He backed away into the shadows, hoping not to be seen.

He kept an eye on the robot outside, wobbling like an unbalanced toy. Step by step, Daniel kept backing away. Barely raising his feet off the floor for fear of kicking or knocking into something. The further in he went, the darker it got.

"Dad?", he whispered. But once again, there was nothing. Just then, his foot came up against the service counter. He spun to duck behind it, but something grabbed him. A hand clamped over his mouth. It took a second to register. It was his father. He let go of Daniel's mouth and held up a finger, warning silence.

A samurai and a marine were brutally pounding away at each other in an apocalyptic city street. Spinning high kicks, barrages of punch combinations and every now and again, the slash of a sword or shotgun blast. Video games had come a long way since Grant had first introduced them to his father. Now, very cinematic on the large screen television in the living room. Clearly a one-sided battle, the samurai's health bar was dropping fast as the marine had him in the corner, pounding away.

And that's when Grant walked in. He watched silently in shock for a moment. No easy thing to startle a former general who *fought in real wars*, but there it was.

"What'cha up to, Dad?"

Sturgess Ford threw the controller, trying (and failing spectacularly) to look casual. "Huh, what? Nothing! I was just... Um I...". On the TV, the samurai took advantage and hacked away at the marine until he collapsed.

<u>**ALLIED GLOBAL DEFENSE ADMINISTRATION (A.G.D.A.) – STOP OVERTHINKING THE COMPLICATED TIMELINE – JUST GO WITH IT.**</u>

World dignitaries and defense contractors were gathered in a vast War-Room type hall, hidden somewhere deep underground, beneath the REDACTED.

Leading the proceedings from a podium in front of a massive wall of monitors was of course, Dr. Stanley Giggs. On the center and largest monitor is the title "G.D.S.N.", because the government lives by its acronyms.

"Ladies and Gentlemen. What we are gathered for today is nothing less than history itself. I am proud to present the fruit of our efforts. The Global Defense Satellite Network!"

The crowd applauded as the surrounding monitors sputtered to life. One showed a spinning globe that highlighted several cities around the world. Others showed schematics and data on the satellites themselves. The rest were all live feed launch site cameras.

"A giant leap for all mankind." And with that he pushed a button. Everybody cheered as they watched the live launches from all the different cameras. The globe showed digital trajectories for no less than a hundred small rockets.

"By using drone technology and artificial intelligence systems with state-of-the-art logic algorithms, we can detect and manage threats from both our own planet as well as outer space. And while we will of course be monitoring them, it will allow us to focus more of our attentions on this!"

With another push of the button, the monitors all joined into one large sectional digital image. "I'm pleased to announce my magnum opus. Not only a central hub to coordinate all the satellites, but over the next several years a team comprised of astronauts from all the countries making up the A.G.D.A. will inhabit this space station. Allowing us to remain hands on as well as further our exploration out into the larger universe!"

FORD RESIDENCE – YOU KNOW THE DRILL

Sturgess Ford sat on the couch wearing boxer shorts and a tank top, wrapped in an old bathrobe. His fuzzy, slipper clad feet rested on the coffee table before him. Beside him, Grant was sharply dressed for work. The way his fingers danced on the game controller buttons was pure artistry. Precise, calm, almost hypnotic. For all the good it did him. His computer-controlled opponent beat him handily.

"How is it that you designed and programmed this game, yet you still suck at it?", the general mocked.

Grant shook his head as he handed over the controller. "It's exactly because I designed and programmed it, that it knows me so well. My patterns and strategies are in the game's DNA."

"Poetic. Then explain how it is that I still don't get you at all". Sturgess began cycling through the menus to start a new match.

Grant checked the time and sighed. I have a meeting. I'll see you tonight."

"Wait. Two minutes. Just sit there, be quiet and let me show you how it's done." His movements were clumsy and ugly by comparison. His arms flailed as if moving the controller actually translated to his character on screen. Grant would have laughed at him, but he was actually destroying his opponent. The very same opponent who he was just crushed by. It was actually more like one minute and twenty-seven seconds when, "Boom! Perfect victory."

This time, Grant did actually laugh. "Well done. Congratulations. What you're doing is called button mashing. No rhyme or reason to it. That's why the computer can't figure you out."

"That's what makes it such a brilliant strategy."

Grant scoffed, "More like an unconscious lack thereof. Are you sure you were really a general?"

"Yeah. And I won then, too."

SOMETIME AFTER TOMORROW

The Survivors' camp was outside the city, in what used to be a suburban wood. Makeshift tents and scavenged equipment were randomly laid out. Clearly meant to be packed and carried off at a moment's notice. There were dozens of people but no electronics to be found. Very few of the residents were elderly, but plenty were sick, injured or just plain starving.

Daniel and Jackson entered the clearing and people began gathering around. "Dad, why don't you go sit down. I'll take care of this."

Jackson laid a hand on his son's shoulder, "Danny…. Sorry, Daniel. I'm so proud of you."

"I know, Dad. You told me already."

"What I mean is, look around, kid. All these people. Most of them can't fend for themselves. They count on us and you've done a great job of taking care of them. Some of them are alive because of you. Your mom would be proud."

The mention of Daniel's mom stung. As much as he tried not to, it showed on his face. "Thanks. It's because of us, not just me. I couldn't do any of this without you. Go rest. I've got this."

After the supplies and meds were all handed out and everybody returned to what they were doing, Daniel found a tree just outside the camp. He climbed up onto a sturdy branch and took his journal from his backpack.

I know dad really means it when he says he's proud. But it almost makes me feel guilty. Sure, the rest of our group needs us, and I'm always going to try to do what I can. But at the same time, I can't help but wonder how this became our responsibility – MY responsibility. And who's responsibility is it to take care of Dad and me?

Mom used to call me an "old soul", but I wonder if that's just because I never got to live in a world where kids watched TV or played video games. Everything I know about electronics comes from studying text books or old instruction manuals. I guess, in this world it's just a good thing that I know how to play hide and seek. How many people are there left like us? How many survivors and do they have to do the same things that we do? I know there are at least a few. I saw them today. I couldn't tell you who they were, or what they look like, but they weren't hiding. They were fighting. I wish we would too. Anything is better than this.

ELECTRO-CON LOS ANGELES

The convention center was packed wall-to-wall with exhibitors, enthusiasts and yes, cosplayers. Everybody wanting to demo the newest hardware and software, buy the coolest collectibles or network themselves. Sections were dedicated to tournaments, booths where fans could meet their favorite streamers or E-sports competitors.

There was a line, several blocks long to enter the auditorium next door. This was where all the biggest companies made their presentations and announcements.

Backstage, the guest of honor paced nervously. He had been here dozens of times in the past. But never like this. Never as the man whose company had taken technology to the next level. This time, he was the main attraction. He could hear the moderator beginning his introduction.

"Ladies and gentlemen. It is my honor to welcome a true revolutionary. For years now, we've all played his games. We love his blog, and the community he's built through his live stream and videos. But now, he's turned our industry on its ear. He's taken gaming off our monitors and put them directly into our heads. A truly immersive experience through his groundbreaking virtual reality technology. Please welcome…"

The crowd erupted even before the name was said. The roar was decibels beyond deafening. "The one and only, GRANT FORD!!"

As he came out from behind the curtain, Grant smiled and waved. On the inside, he was doing his best not to trip and fall on his face. Just trying to take it all in. He couldn't have ever imagined a crowd of thousands all screaming like he was a rock star. To top it all off, right there in the front row, sat his father. Sturgess Ford, general, retired. And he was cheering louder than anyone.

SAN DIEGO PRIMATE PRESERVE

Dr. Jessica Goodwin sat in the clearing of a lush jungle. Yes, in San Diego. She was handing out fruit pieces to the nearly dozen chimpanzees surrounding her.

The chimps all backed off as Hercules, a young silverback gorilla approached giving a loud snort. He plopped down directly in front of her, very close, and held up an upturned palm. Doctor Goodwin gave the large ape a sideways look, "I see. I suppose you want this?" She dangled an apple slice waving it back and forth in front of his eyes. Hercules grunted and tried to take the apple. The doctor quickly snatched it away and held it behind her back. "Uh-uh. Not so fast, big guy. What do you say first?" The gorilla snorted again and turned up his nose in defiance. "C'mon, Herc. You know this. What do you say?" And she slowly moved the apple slice toward her own mouth.

"Ooh! Ooh", shouted Hercules. And then in perfect sign language told her, "May I please have an apple?" Doctor Goodwin grinned playfully. "Why, of course you may, young man", and handed it over. Again, in perfect – and very polite - sign language, he said "Thank you", and gave her a hug that would terrify most people. The chimps all joined in and it quickly turned into playtime.

"Sorry to interrupt".

None of them had seen the older man walk up, but they all stopped and watched as the primatologist / den mother stood and approached him. "I know you weren't expecting me", he said.

"Is this an official visit?" she asked. "Are you here on behalf of the general?"

The man shook his head, "I just wanted to spend a little extra time with them. If you don't mind, that is."

She smiled and shook his hand. "Of Course, Dr. Jepson. You know you're always welcome. They look forward to their time with you. You're family here." And after a long awkward silence, "So, how is he? Have you seen him?"

"Not for a while now. But considering this is General Sturgess Ford, he's likely the same as ever." Dr. Goodwin gave him a knowing nod as she led Jepson to see the apes.

Once again, the A.G.D.A. delegates had gathered. Only instead of the War-Room, they were in what looked a lot like the old N.S.E.P. mission control. Rather than techs in lab coats or uniforms, the work stations were occupied by nerds in flip-flops and tee shirts. Dr. Giggs, once more led the proceedings from a podium in front of a monitor bank. On-screen behind him, the robotic arm from a space shuttle was connecting a final module to a large floating station.

"As you can see, ladies and gentlemen, thanks to these nerd…. um, I mean, these fine engineers, the space station is now complete. All without having to risk a single human life. Even the shuttle is being piloted from right here on this very base. By the time we send up the first team, next week, all systems will be fully functional."

As the last clamp locked into place, and the arm began retracting into the shuttle, everyone in mission control cheered and high-fived.

Dr. Giggs Continued, "Yes, congratulations to us all. A dream come true for sure. But a dream that I could not have realized on my own. Because of the station's fully automated operating system, called Omni 12, we can send up more than just our astronauts. It won't be long before civilian contractors or terra-formers can head for the stars. For that, let me bring up the man we have to thank. The man who wrote the Omni 12 O.S. He assembled the team of programmers you see here, from the finest in the world. Mr. Grant Ford!

SOMETIME AFTER TOMORROW

Daniel was glad that Jackson had finally taken some medicine and fallen asleep. He was careful to stay as silent as possible and not wake his father. Their tent was small and it was dark inside. But Daniel knew exactly what he was looking for. It was in the corner, a small duffle bag that had the word "Mom" written on it in silver marker.

Once outside, Daniel stuffed his journal into the bag and headed off into the woods. This wasn't unusual for him. He knew the area well, so there was no way he'd get lost walking a couple miles from camp. As before, he climbed high up into the branches of a tree. From here, he could almost see the city. Once settled, he opened the bag and began looking through. A few photos, an old coat that still smelled like her, some loose change and at the bottom, an old digital music player.

He knew he shouldn't, but figured that he was far enough from the city that the robots wouldn't be looking for a signal, and if by chance they were, he was far enough from camp that they wouldn't be in danger. He put the buds in his ears and began scrolling through her playlists. He noticed that the charge was getting low, so he likely wouldn't get to do this much more. He found the collection that reminded him most of her and pressed play.

Dad would definitely not be happy if he knew what I was doing. Bad enough that I went so far from camp alone but using an electronic device would give him a stroke. I understand. It's probably stupid but I need this. I miss her every day, and this keeps her close. I remember her singing me these songs when I was little. This is the only way I know to keep going. Anyway, in keeping with things I need and Dad won't like, I have to know who it was attacking those robots. Which means that tomorrow I'm going back out there by myself. So tonight, I get in the zone. Dad worries too much, I'm sure it'll be fine. What could possibly go wrong?

<u>**FORD RESIDENCE**</u>

The general couldn't have been prouder of his son, but ever since he had become so successful, the house just wasn't the same. Their relationship was better than it had ever been, but they just didn't get to spend much time together. He sat on the couch and picked up a game controller, but decided against playing. These days, Sturgess just wandered around like a ghost.

Searching for something productive to do, the former general did his usual rounds. As he passed his office, he noticed his computer powered up. Maybe he had just forgotten to shut down last time he checked the email. But why would the operating system be cycling through lines of code?

On screen, he saw it was actually running a search. "`Classified documents / security access, email - fourstatford@email.gov`".

Sturgess thought that although it was weird, probably still just a glitch. Any codes or passwords he may have forgotten to wipe from the hard drive when he left service would be out of date and useless by now. Just to be on the safe side, he decided to email the base and let them know. But when he tried, he found himself locked out of his old email account.

Mission control was buzzing. It had been some time since the first inhabitants arrived on the space station. Dozens of techs were at their work stations monitoring systems, processing data and running protocols. Until, that is, the power went out. There was a collective gasp followed by panic. Dr. Giggs started shouting, "What is this?!"

From somewhere in the darkness, one of the techs called out, "Sir, we've lost contact with the Space station. We're totally blind!"

Giggs tried to sound calm. "Go to backup systems on the local generator. That's what they're there for."

"Negative, Sir. Backups are down as well."

"The second we get back online, search keystroke histories, any way the systems could have been accessed from the outside. Were we compromised?"

"I don't see how that's possible, sir. We're on a completely closed network and…".

Giggs all but shoved the tech. He was fuming. "Completely closed?! Moron, we're communicating and sharing data with a station floating in space! There are thousands of miles of open air between us and them! So, don't give me that closed network bullsh…."

And then, just like that the lights came back on. Relief would have been an understatement. The computers rebooted and everybody hustled to find that all systems were normal. Giggs was still furious, "This does not happen again on our watch. I want all available personnel looking into what that was!! And somebody get Ford in here! If this is because of his operating system, I swear I'll…"

Thank goodness the printing store was still open at that time of night. Her thesis was due tomorrow and had to look perfect. Of course, she should have been done with it days ago, but her friends were all going out, and she had always suffered from major F.O.M.O. Let's face it, this was far from the first time she had pulled an all-nighter to meet a deadline.

She sat at one of the computer terminals with the coffee she stopped for, even though unsure she'd make it to the printers. There was a moment of panic when she couldn't find the USB drive carrying her paper. Of course, it was all the way at the bottom of her bag.

"Ma'am?", the clerk called out. "We're closing in fifteen minutes."

Even though her phone was buried in the same bag as her drive, she tapped her ear, as if she was on a call, then nodded and waved, hoping he'd leave her alone.

When the girl tried to open her paper in the word processing program, all that came up was random code. "Really?" She tried again. Same thing. She closed the program again and checked to be sure the document was actually on the drive. Sure enough, there it was. "Flat Earth and the Moon Landing Hoax: The Truth Science Doesn't Want You to Know." She tried once again to open it, but still, the same random code.

When in doubt, re-boot. But as the computer came back on, it simply scrolled through code. Oddly enough, the same code that kept coming up as her thesis. No home screen, no desktop. Just code.

"Uh, hey, Mr. copier guy? Yeah, there's something wrong with your computer."

He just shrugged and told her, "So, use another. We have like a dozen of 'em. Ten minutes till closing."

As she moved her stuff to the next terminal, she muttered, "Geez, try to be nice and let a guy know his gear sucks." But this computer was having the same issue. "Seriously? Grrr!" She moved on to the next.... Then the next…. Aaand the next. Same thing on all of them. "Hey, no joke buddy. None of these are working. It's just these stupid lines of code, over and over. A.G.D.A.- launch definition – authorized exe. - fourstarford@email.gov and a bunch of random numbers and letters. Like a non-stop loop."

The clerk didn't leave the desk. "I don't know what to tell you. The manager will be in at ten-thirty tomorrow morning. I'll text him to have it fixed. Come back then."

"But my paper is due at eight am!"

SOMETIME AFTER TOMORROW

Daniel darted from the wreckage of a storefront to the side of a smashed truck. He was always careful of where and when to move, but especially now, alone. He came to the cross-street where he and his father were yesterday and peeked around the corner. After what they had been through here, the quiet was a little spooky. But at least it looked clear.

Keeping low, he moved again. This time to an alley, across from the pharmacy. He checked his surroundings and was reminded of the damaged robot getting back to its feet. But that's what they did. The survivors had learned long ago. Only humans bury their dead. The robots recycle. The damaged ones made their way back to wherever they come from and were either repaired, or the parts are reused to make more robots. The ones that couldn't get back on their own were carried off by the others. Regardless, they didn't seem to be here at the moment.

There, in the street was the tablet he had thrown. Daniel was a little surprised that the robots hadn't taken it. They were scavengers, just like the humans. They collected any electronic bits they could find, again, to make more robots.

Somehow, it was still powered up. A home screen glowed through the sticker for "Mad Squirrels". He had to move. Being this close, he may as well have been jumping up and down screaming "Come get me!" Daniel took a deep breath and bolted. Directly across the street through the broken pharmacy window. Maybe if he could get more supplies, Jackson wouldn't be so angry at him when he got back.

And that was his big mistake. Never go inside anywhere without checking first. Ten feet away sat the damaged robot from the other day. Its huge weapon leveled directly at Daniel's face.

"Can't somebody do something about that alarm?" Mission Specialists and astronauts rushed weightlessly about the operations module of the orbiting station. The small space was deafening until a tech was able to cut the wailing siren.

"Systems report. What're we dealing with here?" The commander demanded. "Engineering?"

"The seals are all good, sir. Life support functioning, levels are a little low."

"Good. Next. Control?"

"Thrusters functioning. Orbital trajectory re-calibrated. Course corrections entered and initiated."

"Tech?"

"Operating system rebooted. The readings from just prior to the event are a bit glitchy, but probably nothing to worry about."

"Everything up here is something to worry about. Define 'glitchy'."

"Yes sir. Sorry, Sir. Response time is lagging and there's a lot of code uploading into the system. For now, it's functional, I'm working on it."

"Communications?"

"We've re-acquired the signal, sir, but the channels are flooded with incoming transmissions."

"What are they saying?"

"Very little verbally, sir. Just that they seem to be back online down there. The rest is digital, looks to be some sort of command code override. Defense system authorization and activation codes. I'm cross-checking it with tech and it seems to be the same data."

"Can you back-trace it to mission control? Maybe cut in to the transmission and speak to them?"

"Negative, sir. The transmission looks like it originates from somewhere off site."

FORD RESIDENCE

Sturgess Ford was in the middle of the living room in his bathrobe. Walking in place, his arms reaching for things that weren't there. The television on the wall showed what he was seeing in the VR glasses he wore. The retired general had actually gotten really good at the games his son had developed before moving into government sector. But today, he seemed to be moving clumsily. The headache was getting worse.

His avatar made its way through the medieval maze, occasionally swinging its sword at attacking demons. The further he moved, the more creatures attacked. Ford tried to duck down a side corridor but found himself unable to move that way. He tried to go back the way he came, but again, nothing. The only way he was able to move, was forward. Each time he tried another direction, his headache intensified. Almost as if the game was delivering shocks to his brain.

There came a pounding at the front door. Ignoring it only made his headache worse. After a moment, he relented, "Alright, alright. I'm coming. Keep your shirt on." He flailed his arms a bit, directing the game to pause, which it refused to do. The demons kept attacking. The knocking at the door was joined by repeated ringing of the doorbell. Finally, Ford simply took off the VR goggles. He couldn't help but notice that his headache immediately faded. "Whoever it is, you're killing my ranking!"

The pounding stopped, "General, we need to speak with you".

Through the peephole, Ford could see the four men in black suits and matching sunglasses. "What's this about," he asked.

"It's important. Can you please just open the door?"

Ford had never liked these types of guys but he opened the door anyway. As he did, the one in front showed his identification. "General, we're with the...". But Ford just walked away from the open door and sat in his chair.

"Yeah, I remember. And I'm not a general anymore. Make it quick, I was in the middle of something."

As the agents entered, one pulled a folded stack of papers from his breast pocket and held it out to Ford. "Sir, this is a warrant to search the property. We'll need to impound all computers and peripheral equipment on the premises."

Ford snatched the papers and tossed them on the table, "Look, I don't care…"

"There was a signal originating from this house, that we believe triggered an event," the agent interrupted.

"An event? Look, I tried to email you about something weird going on with my computer but my account was locked. I thought someone was trying to…"

"Given, the sensitive nature of the work your son's been doing for the government, we just have to do our due diligence. Now please, just stay out of our way."

SOMETIME AFTER TOMORROW

Daniel was dead.

Well, he assumed he was, anyway. Really, how else could it play out? He had bolted into an enclosed space without checking it out. A rookie mistake that landed him face-to-face with the barrel of a gun.

He just stood, time frozen. Thinking about his dad. Thinking about all the other survivors who needed him, who he'd just let down. A million thoughts flew through his head in that fraction of a second. All, set to the classic rock music his mother used to listen to.

Somewhere off in the hazy distance, Daniel thought he could hear the familiar sounds of battle. Braced for his demise, and caught up in his own head, he didn't register the movement from behind the robot. A glint of light in the dusty shadows, and just as the robot's firing mechanism tightened, the weapon flew aside.

The blast blew a hole through the wall and the concussion threw Daniel back out onto the sidewalk.

As disoriented as he was, Daniel still recognized the sound of gunfire and metal banging. He tried getting to his feet to run, but his legs wouldn't respond. Through the dust and smoke inside, he could just make out the small person smashing at the robot with a lead pipe. Rounds from the weapon, pinging around the room. A spark. A bullet must have hit a gas line because there was a blinding flash of light, unbearable heat, and the sound of crumbling brick and metal.

The building was coming down. Again, Daniel tried to scramble. Clumsily he forced himself up, just barely getting to his knees as the first bricks rained down around him. Something crashed into his back, flinging him across the street. Whatever it was, was too big and soft to be stone or metal.

It was in fact, an arm. Well, an arm attached to a person. It dragged him behind the shell of a destroyed car. Daniel rolled onto his back and his eyes went wide. He tried to shout, but the hand clamped down over his mouth. It was Jackson. He held up a finger to quiet his son, then pulled him close and hugged him as tight as he could.

SOGDO MOTORS FACTORY

Sogdo Motors was a young upstart addition to the automotive industry. They were revolutionizing hybrid, fully electric and hydrogen fuel cell technology with self-parking and collision avoidance systems. Even the factory itself was a technological marvel. Very few people were actually on the floor and mainly just to supervise the lines. The actual assembly was being done by machines. Sure, these robots were being controlled by computers, but it took less than an eighth of the staff to program and run than it used to when cars were built by hand.

Of course, the company had been the subject of plenty of controversy. These ranged from humans losing jobs to machines and subverting the normal industry sales conventions such as traditional dealerships. Sogdo favored small store fronts in malls and large online presences. And obviously, the fossil fuel industry was not psyched about losing the business. The upside was that manufacturing overhead was at a minimum, which made Sogdo cars affordable to the public.

The plant floor was immaculate. Cars rolled along conveyor belts from station to station. The chassis were built on one line, the bodies on another. Yet other lines were assembling the engines. As each step was completed, the lines merged with the finished vehicles being moved out by conveyor belt.

Or, that's how it was supposed to work. The belt came to a grinding halt. A car had gotten stuck. Before the lineman could get over and move it, a second car bumped into its rear. Then another and another. The conveyor was a good three feet off the floor, so putting the car in neutral and pushing was out of the question. The lineman waved his arms and shouted at the computer operators behind a large window, "Shut it down! Stop the line."

The jam-up was now six cars deep and quickly growing. The cars were backed up, stuck at the individual lines which had bottle-necked at the merge point. As the computer techs tried desperately to shut it down, the various robots kept bolting and welding whatever was in front of them. Hydrogen fuel cells were being piled one on top of another.

Linemen were frantically trying to find the off-switches on the robots but unable. Large metal arms swung and swatted at the workers. The machines actually seemed to be defending themselves

The computer techs were at a loss as their monitors all showed the same thing: Millions of lines of code, such as:

"Run:

OMNI12.4.7lockoutA.G.D.A.securityprotocolinitiate/fou rstarford@email.gov-

authorize\globaldefense.synch/execute."

One of the robotic arms actually picked up a car body and flung it through the tech room window. The people inside dove and scattered. Sparks flew as equipment was destroyed. The line foreman saw this and had an idea. Shouting into his radio, "Cut all the power to the building! Somebody, get to the breaker panel and shut it down now!"

Lights in the plant began shutting down. Line by line, the robots collapsed. Someone had done it. The circuits were off. The factory was now dark.

Sogdo prided itself on good, solid, reliable construction which really became a problem in that moment. The dozen or so finished cars at the end of the line suddenly started up. They weren't dependent on the building's circuits.

Likely using that self-parking feature, the cars figured out how to shift themselves into gear. They began driving themselves off the side of the conveyor.

Sure, fenders dented and a couple of tires popped, but the cars didn't seem to mind. The workers tried to run or climb up on whatever they could to avoid the cars, which seemed to be trying to run them over.

The foreman actually darted from behind one of the robotic arms and managed to jump into one of the cars. He tried (and failed at) everything he could think of to turn it off. Then he noticed the lines of code, scrolling on the windshield heads up display:

"Run:
OMNI12.4.7lockoutA.G.D.A.securityprotocolinitiate/fourstarford@email.gov-authorize\globaldefense.synch/execute."

"Execute."

"Execute."

"Execute."

Jackson made sure they were far away from any grates or manholes before lighting a flare to see in the sewer pipe. If the robots found them down here, there would be no way to escape. "What were you thinking? You're smarter than that!" He realized that he was near yelling, and quieted to a whisper, "We never travel alone, not to mention without telling anyone!"

"I know, Dad. I just needed…" Daniel leaned against the side of the tunnel, ankle deep in god knows what.

"Needed what?", Jackson cut in, "Look, I'm sorry this is the world you had to grow up in. I'd give anything to change that. But this is what it is. There is nothing you could possibly need bad enough to go running off to the city by yourself."

"Well, it doesn't exactly look like you came with an army either." Seeing the anger and hurt look in his father's eyes, Daniel changed his tone. "Sorry. So, how did you find me anyway?"

Leaning against the wall beside his son, Jackson softened. "C'mon, Kiddo. Give me some credit. I've known you since before you were even an idea. And I knew your mother much longer than that. You're just like her. It wasn't that hard to figure out."

"I needed to try and find whoever that was, fighting the robots."

"They were probably just another pack of survivors. Why?"

"Dad, I've seen them twice now, and both times, they were winning. But that's not the weird thing. They looked like kids. No bigger than me."

"Your eyes must have been playing tricks on you. I can't imagine kids out here fighting them. How could parents…" He noticed Daniel looking at him incredulously with a cocked eyebrow. "Right. Point taken. Present company excluded."

"No. You're missing the point, Dad. Whoever they were, they were winning! What if we joined them? What if we all fought? Maybe we could actually win this war!"

Jackson was crestfallen. "Dan. Believe me, I'd love to hope something like that were even possible. But it's not. You've seen these people twice, in exactly the same place. Whoever this is, is probably just a small group of survivors who've gotten lucky so far, defending what's left of their block. And what about all those people back at the camp? Our people. They count on us…. They count on you. I know you want to help but you can't do that if you get yourself killed. You take care of them by keeping them out of danger. Personally, I'll always see that as the smarter way. And that's how we'll win this war; by being smart."

Daniel knew there was no winning this argument. Not here, in the sewer where his dad had just dragged him after rescuing him, after running away. "I just want to try to make things how they were before the war. Even though I don't know what that really was. Do you remember what it was like back then? Do you even remember how the war started?"

THE BEGINNING

Somewhere in Eastern Europe. Upon first look, you would have been forgiven to think it was some sort of military parade. A column of tanks rolled up a main artery of the city. It was escorting a convoy of heavily armed and plated trucks, but then you would have seen the dozens of little smart cars trailing behind them.

Obviously, nobody was expecting it. The street was crowded with people going about their normal routines. They hurried out of the way as the convoy approached.

Looking even closer, you might have noticed that every one of these vehicles was driving itself. The smart cars looked like contraptions out of some post-apocalyptic movie with fuel tanks and weapons bolted to the hoods, roofs and doors.

Civilian traffic was snarled at an intersection where the convoy suddenly stopped and spread out. A squadron of drones buzzed overhead.

Time seemed to stop. Everybody froze in fear, having no idea what was happening.

But then the world erupted. Tanks and trucks began firing in all directions. People were screaming and running for cover. The drones circled back, releasing bombs from their bellies.

The smart cars revved their engines and started ramming buildings. Their fuel cells and tanks exploding into great fireballs. Smoke darkening the city.

Within minutes, the news outlets were reporting that similar attacks were taking place in cities across the world. And then, the news outlets were gone. Blacked out, much like the cities and mankind itself.

Just like that, the war had begun.

PART 2

CONVERGENCE

Deep underground in the War-Room, all the monitors of the video wall formed a single image. A rotating globe. Much of it covered in growing masses of red. More spots blossoming by the minute.

The chamber was packed wall-to-concrete-wall with delegates from around the world, each blaming another for the attacks. Old grudges bubbling to the surface, alliances falling to pieces. Switzerland sat there quietly minding their business while Canada apologized profusely (for what, no one knew). But nobody (no, not even THEM) was claiming credit for this.

Dr. Giggs stoically took his familiar place at the podium. He tapped the microphone, "Ladies and Gentlemen." But nobody listened. The arguing, if anything, only got louder. "Please, if I could have your attention." Still nothing. Giggs looked to the president of the United States who, along with his staunch cabinet appointees, simply shrugged.

It was finally, the leader of Germany who stepped in. "SHUT UP, YOU GUYS!! QUIET!!" Her voice was so piercing, the microphone squealed with feedback and the room fell silent. She turned and nodded to Giggs.

"Um, yes. Thank you for that, Chancellor." The chancellor blushed and waved at the doctor, making him a bit uncomfortable. "Right. Anyway, we have…"

"Just tell us who is responsible for these attacks", shouted the president of Italy. "Is it terrorists?", asked the Prime Minister of England.

Dr. Giggs held up his hands for silence. "Please. What? No, I don't think this is terrorists. The sheer size of the attacking forces alone negates that possibility. Also, we know that the equipment used in these events comes from all of our own arsenals. I think we need to look at…"

Blunt as usual, the president of France interrupted, "Are you suggesting that the armies of every country in the world are turning on us? Ridiculous! Why are we talking to a scientist anyway? Where are the generals? We should be hearing from them!"

"Monsieur President, I'm trying to get to that point exactly. Please, bear with me." The French president waved a dismissive hand and let him continue. "As I was saying, in this room right now, we have delegates from one-hundred and ninety-three out of the one-hundred and ninety-five countries on the planet. And let's face it, those other two countries, simply aren't capable of something on this scale. No. The reason you're talking to me rather than some general, is because I believe it's a mistake looking for PEOPLE behind these attacks."

"Ah-Ha!", shouted the president of China. "I knew it! It's aliens!"

The president of the United States perked up and turned to his Secretary of Defense, who simply shook his head to stay quiet.

"No!", shouted Giggs, about to tear out his own hair. "It's not Aliens. It's not. As a matter of fact, our scans have shown no sign of biological combatants of any kind. Not a single living soldier... And if any of you idiots asks if it's zombies, I'm going to punch you!" He took a second to compose himself and for dramatic effect "It is my firm belief that we are dealing with Artificial Intelligence."

One of the leaders from South America meekly raised his hand to ask, "So, you think someone is faking this?"

The doctor practically slammed his own face on the podium in exasperation. "Faking? No, why would you? ... Who invited this guy? COMPUTERS!! I'm talking about computers. Good Lord! Is that so hard to believe?

Giggs hadn't felt this frustrated since his computer Chess presentation all those years ago. He stormed from the podium and searched out Grant Ford. "These idiots just don't get it. I need you to come with me. Gather a small detail. We're heading off site."

SOGDO MOTORS FACTORY

The plant floor was no longer the pristine laboratory-like space it used to be. It was now totally devoid of any human life at all. Probably best not to think too much about where they went.

Some of the lines were busy stripping machines of parts. They separated wires, gears, circuits and any other parts that they could salvage.

The assembly lines were still active. More so than ever, in point of fact. Still building vehicles, though very utilitarian looking. All were using the hydrogen fuel cell technology. They ranged from small, light cars for speed, to heavily armored trucks. There were also flying vehicles, both fixed wing and rotors.

As the various lines converged, the new vehicles were each fitted with weapons and computer networking chips.

"Somebody, find that space station!" The project leader screamed.

"Sir, we know exactly where it is. That's not the issue. The problem is that we can't contact them." The project leader leaned over the tech's shoulder and stared at the computer monitor. "Comms are down? How do we fix it?"

"No, sir. Comms are fully operational. It's more like were getting a busy signal."

"What? Billions of dollars in funding, and they don't have call waiting?"

The tech pointed at a scrolling stream of code on screen. "See this? The station appears to be broadcasting. Every frequency and network signal are clogged with this outgoing code."

"Can we see where they're broadcasting to?" The commander asked.

By now, several other techs and officers were gathered around the one work station. The tech frantically punched up data on his terminal. "Sir, it looks like they're broadcasting… Everywhere."

The commander straightened up and thought for a second. "What are they broadcasting?"

And again, the tech just pointed at the screen. "It's all code, Sir. Nothing I've been able to decipher. There's millions of lines of it."

"I want all hands, on deck! Get every available pair of eyes on this STAT! Drag Ford in, this is his system. Somebody figure out what this is. Nobody goes home until we do. In the meantime, I don't care if it means going outside and sending smoke signals, get me in contact with that station!"

It started in the Server-Room. Fans kicked on, one by one. Then an alarm and flashing red light. Everyone froze in place for a second. Then the fans in the computer terminals on the mission control floor started kicking on. "What's this, now?", shouted the leader. And before anyone could hazard a guess, the terminals all began spitting out smoke and sparks. The window into the Server-Room exploded. A second alarm started wailing and all the lights turned red.

Vents in the walls and ceiling began spraying a mist. The commander quickly covered his mouth and nose with his shirt. His shouting was muffled by the cloth. "Everyone out! Halon Fire suppression is active! Don't breathe it in. Evacuate immediately! Go, go, go!!"

<u>LONDON</u>

The streets looked much as they did during World War 2. Buildings were burning and crumbling. Soldiers were taking cover wherever they could find it. Soldiers, wearing the uniforms of many different nations. The Allied Global Defense Army.

Rolling towards their position was a massive convoy of both civilian and military vehicles. They came, side by side, serving as a moving road block. It was as if they were herding the soldiers, pushing them back into the wide-open traffic circle.

The soldiers tried to retreat in the opposite direction. The only hope was to create enough distance that they could scatter and hide. Unfortunately, every street leading to the traffic circle had a convoy of its own. The machines had them boxed in like fish in a barrel.

Above, a squadron of drones moved in and hovered. One by one, bay doors opened, each revealing a payload of bombs. There was no place to run as the bombs began to rain down.

"Captain, we are now passing twelve-hundred meters", the navigator called out. "Approaching crush depth."

Nobody aboard the Russian nuclear submarine had any idea why this was happening. For the time being, all the equipment seemed to be functional... Well, it was all operating, just not responding to the crew.

The captain was trying not to show fear. His crew had to have faith in him if they were going to survive this. Still, each metallic creak of the hull sent chills up his spine. The cold at that depth didn't help much either. And then, of course, there was the pressure.

"Where are we with restoring propulsion?" he asked. The chief engineer shook his head. "Engines are functional, Sir. Just like all other systems. Bow planes are unresponsive and remain at a thirty-degree dive angle."

"Thirteen hundred meters, Sir."

"Is there a way to empty the ballast tanks? Can we jettison any unneeded weight? Dump our munitions and payload? Anything to make this ship buoyant?" At this point the captain was just ticking off the checklist. He suspected the answers but needed to maintain the illusion of productivity in order to hold off the very real fear.

The chief engineer rolled his eyes. He knew what the captain was doing but played along. "Negative, Sir. None of the ports or tubes are responding."

"Thirteen-fifty meters, Sir. Crush depth."

The cracks were beginning to show. Luckily, they were showing only in the captain's demeanor and not yet the hull. "Somebody, give me some good news. What about communications?"

"Negative, Sir. Still jammed. Nothing in or out."

"Fourteen-hundred meters, Sir. Sea bed impact in five..."

The sub rocked as it made contact with the sandy bottom of the ocean. The hull thankfully held, but pipes burst and bolts shot like bullets.

"What happened to four, three, two, one?!" shouted the captain, destroying the last shreds of his false calm. "Okay, what are our oxygen levels? How long can we breathe down here?"

The chief engineer was hesitant to add to the bad news. "Sir, like everything else, the oxygen generators should be working..."

"Yeah, yeah, got it. Don't give me what should-be. Tell me what is! How long?

The engineer was scribbling equations on a note pad. "Best guess? Between nine and twelve hours, Sir"

And then the lights began to flicker.

ALLIED GLOBAL DEFENSE ADMINISTRATION

The wall screens showed battles from around the globe. Every one of them a lost cause. Somewhere in the Middle East, a drone strike was bombing a city. In South America, soldiers were held in a massive group, surrounded by tanks and armored Humvees. In Washington D.C., The Washington Monument toppled from missile fire as a heavily armed column of half-tracks, tanks and smart cars rolled across the National Mall.

The gathered leaders watched in horror as across the world, cars from the Sogdo motors company crashed into buildings, detonating their hydrogen fuel cells. Drones dropped napalm on the decks of naval ships, causing the sailors to dive overboard.

The Russian president shouted out, "We've lost contact with our entire fleet! Someone is taking control and locking us out!"

The Chinese leader followed with, "We just got reports of a massive power spike and then the line went dead!"

Just then, the video feed from South America turned to static. A moment later, North Africa.

The president of the U.S. Slammed a fist on the desk and shouted, "Enough! Find out where these terrorists are coordinating from. I want a missile strike while we still can, pronto!"

The Eastern European feed cut out. One of the techs frantically typed away at his computer. "Sir, there seems to be a coordinating signal, slaving hundreds of satellites around the globe, including our own. We're back tracing it to the space station."

"How many people are onboard?" asked the president.

"Eight currently, Sir."

The room fell silent. They all knew what he was suggesting. P.O.T.U.S. didn't give them the chance to object. "Whoever is doing this has been a step ahead of us this whole time. For all we know one of those astronauts is a mole. I don't like this either but we have a chance to disrupt their signal with a single strike. This is what the A.G.D.A was put in place for. We have to do this now, while we can!"

Slowly, the delegates came around. Silently nodding their consent.

Within moments, missile silos began their firing protocols. Coordinates were entered and the missiles themselves were cycling for launch. "We are weapons hot, sir," informed the tech.

P.O.T.U.S. bowed his head. "Whatever your belief systems are, may they have mercy on us all. Fire at will."

Everybody held their breath as the tech sent the command codes to the missile operators.

Moments felt like hours as they waited for reports. Then finally, "Incoming, Sir. Putting it on speakers."

One by one, the reports came back. In several different languages, but all using many of the same phrases. "Silo door failure." "Internal malfunction." "Evacuate!" Then, one by one, the signals died. Some into a hiss of static, others with a high-pitched electronic whine.

"We've lost the connection," the tech finally admitted.

"Which one," asked one European leader.

"Of the fifty missiles fired? All of them. Bringing up maps now."

The global image confirmed the worst. The launch sites had all been destroyed. Not a single missile had cleared the silos. Instead, they detonated within.

More of a bunker, really. The server room was dark, except for the small blue LED lights on the system. Two soldiers burst through the doors, weapons at the ready. When they were positive that there was nobody inside, they gave the all-clear.

Dr. Giggs and Grant Ford weren't as confident. They stayed low as they entered, making their way through the data banks.

"This one," said Giggs, keeping his voice low. "This is the primary."

Ford took a laptop from his pack and tried to hand it to the doctor who looked scared and confused.

"What are you giving that to me for? You're the software guy." Grant thrust it towards him again.

"But this is your system. I need you to access it. I don't have clearance."

"I can't give you my…"

But Ford cut him off, not even trying to keep his voice down. "Are you kidding me?! Every government on the planet knows we're here. It's not like you're going to get in trouble. They sent us! Just pull up your big boy pants and do it!"

Giggs thought he actually sounded a lot like his father in that moment. "Fine. Right, okay, but don't look at my password."

"What? Just do it. Get me into the admin so I can take control of the system."

The doctor plugged into the server by hardline and checked over his shoulder before entering his password. Of course, Ford peeked.

"Tick-tock, gentlemen", reminded one of the soldiers standing guard.

"There", Giggs said as he handed the laptop back to Grant. "You're in. Just hurry up, no snooping around. Do your job."

Ford was already typing away at the keyboard. "Relax, drgigglepuss01. I'm not looking at your browser history. If I can contact the space station, I might even be able to trace the hack." He typed furiously while the others nervously kept watch.

"Okay, there she is. There's an awful lot of outgoing data coming from them. Hand me the external hard drive from my pack so I can copy it and we can study it later."

"Just hurry up", Giggs chided. This is taking too long. "We need to re-establish…".

"Will you please just shut up and let me do my thing? I just need a second to worm my way past…".

The security system was triggered. Every light in the place started flashing red and the alarm screamed! The four men panicked. The laptop locked up and the monitor filled with a message.

"SECURITY BREACH – DEFENSE PROTOCOL ACTIVATED – SELF DESTRUCT IN 10…9…8…"

Grant and Giggs locked eyes and then together, yelled at the soldiers, "Run!"

The soldiers were clearing their exit, and Grant turned back from the door to see the doctor still fiddling with the laptop. "Leave it! We have to get out!"

Giggs finished what he was doing and slammed it shut. They had to run like crazy to escape before the room was engulfed in flame.

SOUTHWEST SATELLITE ARRAY

Amidst acres and acres of open field stood hundreds of huge satellite dishes. All lined up uniformly in rows, like a battalion of soldiers at attention. Well, all but the one.

That's what had dragged the maintenance guy away from the big game and out from the warm office, four stories below ground. He had taken this job specifically because it was boring and he rarely had to deal with people.

Dish number 178 was out of alignment. The signal light on the office console had started flashing. He would likely have ignored it, but knew that if he didn't go check it out, he'd start getting phone calls. And taking the ride out into the field was most definitely more preferable than talking to those government science guys.

Obviously, not just anybody could fix these things. You had to have expert knowledge and skills. So, of course, the first thing the maintenance worker did when he got out of his truck was give the base a good hard kick. Oddly enough, it did nothing. Next, he walked around the base of the dish, checking to see if maybe the gears had gotten clogged or the wind had blown it out of alignment. When he was finally sure that actual work couldn't be avoided, he grabbed his toolbox and opened the wiring panel.

All the connections seemed tight and solid, so he moved on to the fuse panel. Nothing looked scorched or broken. When in doubt, reboot. He flipped off all the breakers, counted to five-Mississippi and flipped them back on.

From above came the sounds of metal cogs moving. That must have done the trick. He took a step back to make sure it was lining up. Only, it wasn't. It wasn't moving at all. Dish number 123 was moving. And then Dish 046, followed by 092. And soon enough, all the dishes were moving out of alignment. Once they stopped, it looked completely random to him.

This was going to take time to figure out and fix. There would be no getting around that. He took out his cell and tried to call in the report.   He had no reason at all to expect that standing in the middle of a massive field of satellite dishes, there would be no signal, but... there it was.

He drove back to the office and tried again from a hard line. The call failed and he thought, *Well, at least that means they probably can't call me either.* He decided instead to just email them. That way, he could also check the dish feeds. Two birds, one stone.

The computer terminals were on the fourth level. As he brushed away the mountain of fast food wrappers and fired up the computer, he wondered if anybody had ever been so clever and efficient as he was.

The monitors came online, and all of them showed the same map of the satellite array. Every dish was showing red. He tried to minimize the display so he could email, but the system wouldn't respond. Along the bottom of the screen was the message, "Initiating sequence 2. Transmitting data."

SOMETIME AFTER TOMORROW

Daniel was once again up in his tree on the outskirts of camp. His mind was turning in restless circles that made it impossible to sleep. Well, that and the adrenalin, still coursing through him from the narrow escape earlier.

He knew that his father was right. He had to be smart if they were going to survive. But again, shouldn't being smart also include making progress? Hadn't he always heard people say, "Fortune favors the bold and luck favors the prepared?" Yet here he was being told to play it safe.

He had to calm down. Try to shut off his brain for a few hours and get some sleep. There was no way to be either smart or bold if he collapsed to exhaustion. He kept a very specific playlist of music for just these moments. Old rhythm and blues. More of his mother's favorites. It didn't take long at all for him to doze off up in the branches, high above the forest floor.

That was most likely why he didn't hear the growing rumble in the distance. The sounds of cracking branches and scared animals fleeing was lost, as in his ears someone sang about better days.

ALLIED GLOBAL DEFENSE ADMINISTRATION WAR-ROOM

A line of aides was bringing in small, shoe box-sized machines and setting them up around the room. Others followed with spools of cable, which were then attached to the machines.

The wall monitors all showed maps of nuclear missile launch sites from around the world. By the minute, more and more lit up with words beneath them like "Armed, online," or "Ready for Launch." And right in the center was, "Sequence 2, initiated."

"Make no mistake, Comrades," said the Russian president. "Every one of those missiles is under the command of our mysterious enemy. This is life or death and I fear, the last chance to stop this before full scale global war. If anybody in this room has any information about who may be doing this or why, now is the time to speak up."

Everybody looked around the room waiting for someone else to speak up. The War-Room had never been so quiet.

It was the U.S. president who broke the silence. "One way or another, we know that every signal of a digital nature is being hacked. Systems blocked, and communications lost. That's why we've brought in the telegraph machines. From here on out, we operate analog only."

"But how will we use our weapons? They're all networked," shouted someone from the back.

"Haven't you been listening? We have no weapons! They've taken over everything. Our priority is survival! Contact your people. I want every scientist and computer geek on the planet working on this! Find Dr. Giggs. I want him here, now! And someone figure out what Sequence 2 means!"

SOGDO MOTORS FACTORY

There were no more vehicles rolling off the assembly line. All the scrap parts they had collected and sorted were now being used to build robots. All shapes and sizes. Some using the old machinery from the line itself. Some had legs and others, the treads from tractors or tanks. All were armed to the proverbial teeth. This was Sequence 2 and it was happening in factories all over the planet.

SOMETIME AFTER TOMORROW

Daniel clung tightly to the trunk as the tree violently shook. Luckily, he was hidden high up in the canopy as the robots passed below. He wanted more than anything, to jump down and help those in the camp, or at the very least, somehow warn them. But his father's words came back to him, *I know you want to help, but you can't do that if you get yourself killed.*

It was excruciating to just stay put, especially since this was likely his fault to begin with. Whether it was his running off to the city or even more likely, his using the digital music player. One way or the other, he had led the robots right to the camp.

And then the screaming began. It came directly after the weapons fire started. He could hear the other survivors running to escape the attack. Clearly, not all of them would make it. If he had been closer, at least he would've been able to see. But here, in the tree canopy, so far away, all he could do was listen.

Far below, he saw a woman running with a child in her arms. Then an older, out-of-breath man. More and more people. none of which were his father. The blasts grew louder still. The robots were chasing them. Daniel wanted to scream for them to climb up into the trees and hide but he was helpless, paralyzed with fear.

These people, the only ones Daniel had ever really known, would never get away. He had to do something. He realized he still had the music player and was again reminded that this was his fault. Hitting "Play", he turned up the volume as loud as it would go and threw it as far into the woods as he could.

FORD RESIDENCE

You could hear the engine from almost a mile out. Nothing to be done about that. Ever since he was a young boy, Grant Ford had been enamored with classic muscle cars. How lucky was that? Loud as it was, the car was from a time before GPS or Bluetooth systems. No computerized fuel systems or sensors at all. Not even plastic bumpers, just a ton of steel, a battery, gas and oil. When the money started coming in, Grant bought it from the junk yard and restored it with his own two hands, using nothing but original parts. It was in pristine condition, Grant's baby. One has to wonder what those who gave him flack for not driving a hybrid would say about it now.

Grant and Dr. Giggs took the corner at break-neck speed and skidded to a stop in front of his father's house. Metal storm shutters were all rolled down covering the windows. The general didn't answer when the pair knocked and rang the bell. Cautiously, Grant used his key.

Inside, the lights were all off, as were the clocks on the home theater and microwave. Giggs flipped the light switches on and off a couple of times. "Looks like someone turned off the power."

The pair walked through the house, calling for the general. Still, no reply. Using a flashlight, they checked the basement. Nobody there either, but the fuse box confirmed that someone had indeed turned off all the power to the house.

The general's car was still in the detached garage, a layer of dust suggesting that it hadn't been driven in a while. "Where would he go?" the doctor. asked. "Maybe a neighbor's house, or a friend?"

Grant thought it over for a minute. "I'm not sure he has any real friends, and he never liked the neighbors. He calls them soft and entitled. He's not a very social guy."

A thump from above startled them both so they ducked behind the car. Grant whispered, "Hobby room, above us."

They snuck outside and around back up the stairs. No sooner had Grant reached to knock when the window beside him exploded from a shotgun blast. Grant hit the deck, screaming, "Dad! Stand down, It's me... Your son!"

Inside, the shotgun racked another round. "Are you alone?"

Looking over his shoulder, Grant saw that Giggs had jumped or more likely fallen down the stairs. He looked relatively unhurt, brushing himself off. "No, Dad. Doctor Giggs from the A.G.D.A is with me."

The door flew open and General Ford yanked his son in. "What is this? Did they send you? They think I did this? I had nothing to...".

"Dad, stop." Nobody thinks you did anything. I need you to come with us."

"Where?"

Doctor Giggs stepped through the open door. "You almost killed me!"

The retired general shrugged, "What can I tell you? I'm a little rusty. What's all this about?"

"Computers are going offline all across the globe. Somebody is hacking the world's military. They've been one step ahead at every turn. Haven't you seen the news? We need you to come to the A.G.D.A."

Ford retreated and raised the gun again. "I knew it! They think it's me and they sent you to take me in! How many guys did they send with you? Just let them try!"

Grant shoved the gun aside. "Knock it off, would you? Every military on the planet is based on computers. Those computers are being used against us. How many times have you told me that you fought in *real wars*? The world needs someone who knows how to fight back in analog! The world needs you!"

A.G.D.A. SPACE STATION

Red lights were flashing and alarms beeping. Every monitor aboard the station was displaying the same message, "INITIATE LAUNCH SEQUENCE."

The entire crew was frantically trying to figure it out. Communications specialists tried in vain to contact the Earth below while techs tried to hack the system. Engineers and control specialists desperately poured through the station's manuals and specs.

The commanding officer stormed over to the techs. "Why can't we just reboot the system?"

To which the tech shook his head and answered, "Sir, we can't even get into the system. It's locking us out at every turn."

Turning to the engineers, the CO shouted. What about the power. Can we pull the plug or something?"
The engineers all looked to one another, not saying a word before the lead shrugged. "We can disconnect the power cells manually but that would include life support. We'd be without it for as long as it takes to restart."

"How long is that, exactly?" Again, the lead engineer looked to his compatriots who all shrugged. "I can't give you an exact time. Best guess? Anywhere from twenty minutes to an hour."

The commanding Officer sighed. He was silent for a moment before addressing everyone aboard. "Suit up. I want everyone in EVA suits right now. We're shutting it down." And then he poked a finger into the Engineer's chest. "You have thirty minutes. After that, the EVA's run out of oxygen and we all die. No pressure... Literally."

Once the crew were suited up, the commander addressed them again over the PA system. "Listen up, people. The engineers are heading down to the station's guts. Tech crew will stay here with me in control to oversee the start-up. Anybody not directly involved with resetting the system, I want you to stay in the cargo hold. Strap in if you can, otherwise just hold onto something. This will likely affect our orbital trajectory. We don't know how long this reboot takes, so I want each of you looking out for the person standing beside you. We're in uncharted waters here, but you've all been trained for space, which includes preparing for the unexpected. I would have liked to tell you to make the world proud, but we need to aim higher. So, instead, I'm reminding you that it's our job to keep the planet safe."

*****

The mechanical corridor was small. Even smaller, with the engineers in their bulky EVA suits. The head of the department finished unscrewing the circuit panel. Inside was a master switch. "Commander? We're ready down here."

From his helmet's earpiece he heard the commander, "We're as ready as we'll ever be. On your count. Do it."

The engineer gave his team a quick nod before closing his eyes. "Sir, shutting down in three… two… one." And he threw the switch.

The lights flickered… and then nothing. That's not to say the systems went off. Nothing in fact changed. The lights, the oxygen filtration, the computers all kept working. "Maybe it takes a second?" he said. After nearly twenty seconds, he tried flipping the switch on and then off again. Same thing. Just a flicker and continued functionality.

Again, from his ear came the commanding officer, "We doing this, or not?"

"Well, sir, we seem to have a problem. The system won't shut down."

"How is that possible?", the commander shouted. The engineers all looked at each other, blankly shrugging.

Finally, it dawned on him and the lead suggested, "Sir, we failed to account for the emergency back-up power."

In the control module, the commander was furious. "Failed to account? WE DON'T HAVE THAT LUXURY!! Our crew is burning through their portable oxygen supplies. Hurry up and shut down the back-up system!"

86

"That's the problem, sir. We can't do that. It's a fail-safe. Think of this station like a cell phone, taking power from a wireless charger."

"Can we jettison the solar panels?", asked the commander.

"Wouldn't solve the problem. They've been collecting and storing power since launch. The station would probably operate on back-up for almost a month."

The commander yanked off his helmet. "That's just perfect! Of all the times for the government to be efficient!"

Every monitor in the room was showing a different news broadcast from around the globe. The delegates were lined up at rows upon rows of telegraph machines. Relaying messages to and from their respective countries. None of them seemed to have given nor received any sort of good or even encouraging news.

Dr. Giggs stormed in, flanked by Grant and General Ford.

The general and the U.S. president immediately locked eyes. The last time they had seen each other was in Ford's office, with the general being forced into retirement.

After long seconds, the president broke the silence, "Where have you been and what happened at the outpost?... And why in the world is HE here?", gesturing to the general.

"They said you sent for me, that you needed me!", the general shouted back.

The president was stunned, "Why would we possibly need you? A washed-up old relic who..."

"Old?" The general fired back. "You got so fat and gray that I didn't even recognize..."

"Shut up! Both of you!" Grant interrupted. "No. They didn't send for you, but they…We most definitely need you."

"In case you haven't noticed," The president argued, "this is a software issue. Your software! Not some skirmish in some jungle or desert!"

"You're wrong, Sir," Giggs interrupted. "All due respect, but look around you. Our enemy has been so effectively using all the machines against us, that we've had to resort to Jurassic technology like telegraphs. Our troops are being slaughtered out there. I don't think Tech Support is cutting it. After the outpost went sideways, Ford and I decided we needed a different approach."

"Sir," one of the aides called out. "You need to see this." One by one, each of the broadcasts (all of them telling people to find shelter) turned to static.

SOMETIME AFTER TOMORROW

It was no use. The robots had only been distracted by the digital music player for a few seconds. Maybe one or two people were able to escape. But far too many others were being grabbed and dragged off.

The noise below, however, was enough to allow Daniel to follow, staying high up in the dense canopy. As the terrified survivors passed beneath, he searched every face for a sign of his father. Each look of horror, each scream and every single tear streaking their faces only made Daniel angrier.

He was beginning to fall behind the pack. Traveling across the branches wasn't easy.

Bringing up the rear, a robot was carrying a woman by the collar of her coat. She kicked and flailed, trying to get away but the robot had her dangling a foot off the ground, allowing her no leverage. She reminded Daniel of his mother and that was all he could stand.

Daniel launched himself down onto the robot's back, his arms around its neck. The clamps which served as the machine's hands were both full. One with the poor woman who was starting to strangle, and the other with a gun. It tried to swat at Daniel, but couldn't get an angle on him. Round and round, they all spun as they grappled.

For his part, Daniel slapped uselessly at the mech's domed head. "Unzip your coat and raise your arms," he screamed to the woman.

Dazed and in agony, she struggled trying to do as he said. Halfway down, the zipper got stuck.

He kept pounding away, aware that he was at best a distraction. The robot fired his weapon and missing by just inches. Again, its arm, unable to get a proper firing position. But that's when Daniel saw it.

Just then, the woman's zipper gave way. She flung her arms up over her head and slipped out. A huge metal foot almost crushed her as she hit the ground.

"Now, Run!" Daniel yelled at her.

The robot scanned the empty jacket in its clamp, giving Daniel his opportunity. There was a gap in the plating between the upper arm and the shoulder. Daniel reached in and grabbed a handful of wires, yanking them free. Sparks flew and circuits sizzled. Daniel was barely able to roll out of the way as the robot toppled backwards.

In over a hundred countries across the globe, klaxons wailed as missile silo doors began sliding open. Naval ships began pulling out of port under their own power. In Hawaii, an aircraft carrier actually ripped the dock from the pilings of the island itself. Sailors abandoned ship wherever they could. A lucky few made it into inflatable life rafts. Most simply jumped over the sides into the water.

Submarines surfaced, their launch tubes opening. Off the coast of China, one crew bravely tried to scuttle the vessel, instead, only trapping themselves on the lower decks beneath sea level.

The last place you would want to be was this close to any of the planet's largest military bases. And yet, San Diego was also a city, packed with tourist destinations. Rather an apt illustration of humanity's forethought.

Less than ten miles away, Doctors Jepson and Goodwin, along with a handful of trainers, were shepherding apes and monkeys of all sizes and species into a concrete building to the lab level, three stories underground.

In cities and small towns everywhere, people were hurrying to find shelter in basements, bomb shelters and even subway stations. Among them was a much younger Daniel, being carried by his father, Jackson, as his mother struggled to keep up.

SOMETIME AFTER TOMORROW

The robot was flopping around like a fish out of water. From his hiding spot behind a large tree trunk, Daniel spotted its weapon on the ground. As quick as he could, he darted out, grabbed the gun and ducked behind another tree. It was heavier than he had expected. What was a handgun to the robot was more the size of a rifle in the boy's arms.

Daniel had to believe that between the noise and the robot not being where it was supposed to, the others would likely circle back. He pushed the muzzle of the gun against the back of the robot's head where presumably the CPU was housed. The trigger took a lot of strength to squeeze. The blast was deafening in his ears and the blowback, even worse. Daniel was launched backward off his feet.

As quickly as he could, Daniel got up and ran off into the woods. But instead of escaping, he chased after the others. The metal creatures were clearly intelligent, but they weren't human. As such, they weren't very clever. They could adapt, but they couldn't very well improvise. That was Daniel's advantage. He knew these woods well enough that he could easily hide and not be locked onto. Where possible, he used trees or large rocks to brace the weapon while picking off targets.

The robots had formed a perimeter in a clearing that the survivors had been using for water collection. Dumpsters, barrels and large drums, lined with plastic to catch the rain, were scattered about. Some were leaking water where bullet holes had torn through. Several of them had been flipped on their sides or completely overturned.

Doing his best to stay hidden, Daniel circled the clearing, searching for a safe place to attack. Off to one side, he came upon a dumpster, upside down with one end propped up on a boulder. It was just what he was looking for. Dropping to the ground, he belly-crawled as fast as he could under the dumpster's edge. Once inside, he turned around to make sure he hadn't been spotted.

Reasonably satisfied, he began to shimmy himself backward to the dark end. About halfway, his foot kicked something that he just assumed was a thick root. How wrong he was. As he tried sliding around it, the thing reached out and grabbed his leg. Before he even realized it was happening, Daniel screamed.

A.G.D.A. SPACE STATION

Desperate and helplessly trapped, the crew milled about searching for any small spark of hope. What they found instead was first spotted by the communications officer who had been staring out a porthole.

The Earth seemed to be encircled in a growing spider's web. Thousands of thin white threads which originated from the surface, were wrapping themselves around the entire planet. "Sir, I think you need to see this".

The commander moved in to look, and his jaw went slack. "Good Lord! Contrails."

"Beg your pardon, sir?", asked the communications officer.

"Those are contrails... Missiles. You're looking at missiles launching."

"Who's firing them?"

"From the looks of it? Everyone. And it may very well mean that even if we do figure a way to get off this station, there won't be a planet to go back to."

ALLIED GLOBAL DEFENSE ADMINISTRATION WAR-ROOM

Safely tucked away in the bunker far beneath the surface, all the delegates were staring in awe at the massive monitor on the wall. It seemed to be the last one able to receive anything other than static. The aides and administrators were desperately trying to maintain contact with their homelands.

General Ford sat in a far corner, his back to the concrete wall, defeated. Grant walked over, sat beside him and asked, "You okay, Dad?"

The general shrugged. "I don't even know how to answer that. It's not that I don't appreciate you bringing me down here, but we're too late."

"Could be worse," Grant replied. "I'm the guy who designed the system. I'm in no small way responsible for this. So, stop whining, soldier. Pull up your big boy pants and get ready to fight!"

The general was stunned. "What? Can you not see the big TV over there? The missiles are in the air, and in a few minutes everything we've ever known is going to be destroyed. Everything I've ever fought to protect, and all I can do is sit down here and watch."

"All due respect, Dad, but knock it off. Sure. Admittedly, this missile thing is bad. But they were useless to us anyway since the system was hijacked. And hey, on the bright side, they can only use them once, right?"

"Did you really just say that?"

"Yeah, sorry. Bad joke. I tend to do that when I'm nervous. But there are going to be survivors, and they're going to be scared and desperate. We can't just give up. And that's why Giggs and I came and got you."

"And here I thought it was because I'm your father and you were worried."

"That too. But I have a plan. Okay, more of an idea really. An idea that you gave me. But if it's going to work, I'm going to need you to pull it together, soldier. Now, can you do that?"

SOMETIME AFTER TOMORROW

Daniel kicked wildly at the thing holding his ankle while trying to get away. He leveled the weapon, but it was hard to see in the darkness and he was afraid to blow off his own leg.

"What's wrong with you? You should have run!", came a voice from the inky blackness.

"Dad? Oh my God! Dad, are you okay? I couldn't find you and this is all my fault and…"

"Daniel, shut up! They'll hear you. Look, you need to get away. I'll distract them while you run."

"No way! I'm not letting them take you! I got one of their guns. We'll shoot our way out. I know my way through these woods, and…"

"Stop. Quiet, they'll hear us. Give me the gun, and you run as fast as you can into the woods and hide."

"Dad, no. I won't leave you! Come with me. If we're quiet, they won't…"

And just then, the dumpster flew off of them, momentarily blinding them in daylight. "Dad, get behind me!" Daniel raised the weapon, ready to fight and if need be, die to protect his father. But as his eyes cleared, he saw that they were completely surrounded by robots.

<u>EARTH</u>

Almost like a well-choreographed fireworks display, the missiles found their targets. Bright blossoms of flame erupted across the globe. The debris thrown up from the explosions choked the atmosphere and shrouded the planet in dust clouds and smoke.

*****

The astronauts watched from their front row seats in low orbit aboard the space station. And then the shockwaves started to hit.

ALLIED GLOBAL DEFENSE ADMINISTRATION WAR-ROOM

The bunker shook like an eight-plus earthquake. Shelving and whatever else wasn't bolted in place crashed to the floor. The delegates were all screaming and hiding beneath desks and tables. Monitors fell from their wall mounts, shattering. The large one, held on, but now showed only static. The swinging overhead lights flickered and shut off.

Seconds later, the emergency power kicked in, and mounted lights in the corner bathed the room in a blue glow.

Once the world finally stopped bouncing and the noise subsided, the general was the first to stand up. He immediately took note that they still had power. Why that was important stayed just outside his grasp. But it was, he knew for certain.

Little by little, all the representatives emerged. And as is human nature, they immediately began blaming one another. The Italians blamed England who in turn blamed India. The Chinese blamed Russia and the United States pushed off blame on everybody. Off to one side of the bunker, a fistfight broke out. The North Korean leader actually stepped in between Canada and Switzerland before they could kill each other.

And that seemed to be just the kick in the pants that General Ford needed. "Enough!" He slammed a fist on the table, immediately silencing everybody. "Our planet is burning out there. The whole planet. Go ahead and let that sink in for a minute. One way or another, it doesn't matter who pushed the button, because all of you in here are responsible. How could you let it get this far?"

"That's just it," Giggs spoke up. "I tried to explain, I don't think anybody pushed the button at all."

The Chinese delegate jumped in from there. "And It's definitely not the aliens either."

Giggs facepalmed before continuing. "The only thing that makes sense is that it's the computers themselves."

Ford looked at his son. "So, you really weren't kidding when you said this was your fault?"

Grant blushed. "No, Dad... I mean, General... I mean, Sir. Whatever. The point is, Giggs is right. I know how it sounds, but look at it logically. We taught the machines everything we knew. Gave them all our operating manuals and strategies. We made their brains better than ours, and they just kept learning. They figured out our patterns, Dad. Don't you see?"

The general sighed deeply. "You mean like the video games?"

Grant nodded, "Far more complex than that, but yeah, like the video games."

"And that's why I'm here? That's your plan?"

With a shrug, Grant admitted, "It's not much, but it's the best we've got. We're predictable. We need to start button-mashing."

Blocking his father from the closing robots, Daniel sprayed bullets in an arc. "If I can clear a path, you have to run, Dad. Get into the woods!" But his efforts seemed futile. For every robot that he took down, another seemed to fill the gap. Although they didn't return fire, they were closing in.

"You should have just left me!" Jackson shouted over the noise. "I don't think we're getting out of this".

"You can't just give up, Dad! Do something! Can you reach one of the fallen one's guns?"

But it was no use. There was no way for Jackson to get one without being grabbed by the robots. And then things went from bad to worse. Daniel's weapon clicked empty.

"NO! No, no, no, no! Don't do this!" He let the weapon drop to the ground, and put up his hands as the robots closed in. "I'm sorry, Dad. At least we're together in the end.

"Hopefully we at least bought the others some time to get away." Jackson put an arm around his son, preparing for the inevitable.

ALL ACROSS THE GLOBE

The entire planet seemed shrouded in thick smoke and debris. In every major city, the robots moved through the streets in a sweeping pattern. They were searching. Uninterested, for the moment at least, in human survivors. They sifted through the rubble for anything useful. Circuit boards, batteries metal and even plastic. They worked in well-organized units.

Scrap yards, factories and recycling plants were the primary targets. Much like one would assume grocery stores and pharmacies would be to humans. When the robots finished with those, they moved on to the rest.

The robots looked as diverse as the humans themselves. Some were small and sleek, built for maneuverability while others were large and utilitarian, built for demolition and heavy lifting. Others still, were designed to pull the wires and cables from beneath the streets and building walls, with large spools on their backs to wind it all neatly.

In the skies above were drones, coordinating the search missions through wi-fi networks. Most were appropriated from our world's militaries while others were clearly built specifically for the takeover

The other end of those wi-fi connections was miles and miles above the planet's surface, aboard the commandeered space station. The hostage astronauts were helpless. At this point they mostly just concentrated on staying alive and keeping their muscles from atrophying in the zero-gravity environment.

It became sort of an unspoken rule that they did not watch the monitors for fear of going mad at the sight of stolen data scrolling past. If that data had been biological, it would have been described as mutating. Financial institutions, social networks, defense and military servers, gaming networks. The computer was absorbing it all, rearranging the formulas into something new. It streamed the new code down to the robot army, arming them also with the very virtual reality system developed by Grant Ford.

Every one of them were now capable of seeing, interacting with, and adapting to any environment on the planet. "O.M.N.I. SYSTEMS - UPGRADE COMPLETE."

ALLIED GLOBAL DEFENSE ADMINISTRATION

Days had passed. The bunker had done its job withstanding the blast, but the world around it was scorched and in rubble. The smoke and dust were still too thick to see at any distance. The ground itself still burned in several spots.

A team in hazmat gear searched the area. The scientists carefully scoured the grounds with Geiger counters and radiation detectors while the soldiers formed a perimeter in case the robots showed up to finish the job.

Upon returning to the bunker, the team had to pass through a full decontamination chamber where they peeled off their Tyvek suits. Once cleared, they were shepherded into the elevator leading nearly a mile below ground.

Once they finally reached the War-Room, the delegates all gathered around for their briefing. "The bad news is total destruction out there. The closest impact to us was about a quarter mile to the southeast. We found a crater, which suggests that detonation occurred upon impact, rather than in the air."

"And that means what, exactly?", asked the Canadian Prime Minister.

"Actually," the scientist continued. "That would be the good news. If they were using biological weapons, they would likely have detonated them in the atmosphere for airborne disbursement."

The German delegate chimed in. "It makes sense. Any bio-agents would have been useless. They would have either been vaporized by the blast or neutralized by the nuclear radiation anyway. They knew not to waste it."

"That's more good news." The scientist kept going. "There's no trace of radiation at all. I mean, between all the smoke and dust in the air, I wouldn't be in a rush to go out there, but once it settles, it'll be perfectly breathable."

The president of the United States was confused. "Are you saying that they didn't arm the nuclear warheads? Why would they do that? I would totally have armed the nukes. Sounds like our enemy is weak."

"We don't know why yet, Sir. But they've been smart and efficient this whole time. I think it would be foolish to underestimate them by not assuming they had a specific reason."

And as all the delegates began debating and shouting above one another, General Ford was running the information over and over in his head. He saw his son and Dr. Giggs talking off to the side, and that's when it occurred to him.

The robots bulldozed through big cities and small towns alike. They herded the humans like cattle, marching them off to who knows where, or even why. Those who couldn't keep up were…. Well, you know. It was gross, you don't want to know. Those who could, did their best to help the others in hopes of avoiding those consequences.

A loud rumbling shook a small community church that already looked close to collapsing. The cellar door creaked open and a woman peeked out. "I don't see anything, but we have to move quick. I can hear them coming."

Pushing the doors fully open, she helped the other survivors get up the steps to the surface. There were maybe thirty in all, including a young woman and her husband, Jackson. Cradled in his arms was their young son, Daniel.

But they were moments too late. A squad of robots broke through the tree line. The people scattered for the woods. Few of them made it. Daniel was screaming in his father's arms and wriggling his body, slowing Jackson down. They weren't going to make it.

The young mother saw this and without hesitation spun in her tracks. "Hey, Microwave! Over here!" She picked up a large rock and hurled it at the closest robot. "Look at me! What are you waiting for?"

Jackson heard his wife and stopped. "What are you doing? Stop…. I mean, Run!!" But you never mess with a lioness protecting her cub. She picked up another rock and continued taunting the metal creatures as she pelted them.

"Jackson, go! Get Danny out of here! GO! I'll catch up."

Jackson knew she wouldn't, but he had no choice other than to protect their son. As they ran into the woods, Daniel sobbed and kept calling out for his mother.

"I have a plan," the general said.

He was in a corner of the bunker with Grant and Dr. Giggs, who replied, "Then you need to be sharing it with the delegates. Not whispering it to us in the dark."

"It's more of an idea, really. You're idea, Grant, actually. It's going to sound absolutely bonkers to these people, so I'll need your help pitching it."

"I'm in," said Grant.

But the Doctor wasn't quite as eager to commit. "I'm listening. If it's viable, I'll do what I can."

The general rolled his eyes. "Fine. Dr. Giggs, I'm sort of surprised that you haven't figured this first part out yet. You are the tech-guy, after all." This time it was the doctor who rolled his eyes before motioning for Ford to continue.

"The nukes. Everybody here is trying to figure out why. If the robots…"

"Artificial Intelligence," Giggs interrupted.

"…Whatever. If the machines want to exterminate us, why didn't they arm the nukes?" The others shrugged. "Really? Nothing? Heck of a scientist you are. They're not trying to keep us alive, they're trying to keep themselves alive…. Or running." And still, blank stares from the other two. "The nuclear blast produces an electro-magnetic pulse. Don't you get it? They couldn't risk destroying themselves!"

"And so, what's this idea of yours; Or, mine? Whatever," Grant said.

"It's obvious, really. Just like your video games. Everything they know, they learned from us. They're reading us like an algorithm. Our patterns and processes allow them to anticipate each move we make, before we make it. If we're going to stop this, we can't keep thinking like humans!"

"And so?" the professor pried.

"I need to get a message to someone."

AFTER TOMORROW

Daniel and Jackson knelt in the clearing, hands on their heads in defeat as the robots closed in. A circle of weapons leveled at their heads. It was over.

NOT!

From the tree tops and behind rocks and rubble, something… Dozens of somethings, attacked the robots. They were the same ninja-like soldiers that Daniel saw in the city. But they weren't all small. They varied in both size and shape. The biggest of them was nearly seven feet tall with long powerful arms.

Jackson used the distraction to grab his son and run into the brush. Daniel took cover behind a rock and tried to watch the fight. "Hey, what are you doing?" his father whispered. "We have to keep going. We have no idea who these people are. C'mon."

Daniel ignored his father, caught up in the battle. They all wore tactical gear including riot helmets with tinted visors. The way they moved was incredible. So quick, strong and agile, the machines didn't know what hit them. Some of them had guns, while the rest used their hands and rocks to smash them to pieces.

When it was over, the soldiers went about dismantling the robots and collecting their weapons and ammunition. Daniel knew they should get out of the area, but he just needed to see who these guys really were.

Finally, Jackson took Daniel by the arm to lead him away, but it was too late. As they turned, they found themselves face to face with one of the big ones. It took a second to realize what they were seeing. He was no longer wearing the helmet. And when he exhaled, Daniel and his father got a full whiff of its gorilla breath.

The rest of the soldiers now gathered around and began removing their helmets. Several different species, yet all ape. Each uniform had the same insignia. The National Space Exploration Program.

PART 3

TAKING BACK THE PLANET

SOMEWHERE IN LOUISIANA

Weeks had passed since the initial attack. Food supplies had grown scarce. The robots had been smart enough to destroy grocery stores and farms. People were forced to sneak out in small scavenging parties.

What were left of the military forces began going out on search and rescue missions, looking for survivors. Since modern vehicles relied on computer technology, they had reverted to old, World War Two-era trucks. The problem with those, however, was the noise. They adapted by putting the vehicles in neutral and using horses and oxen to pull them.

They only moved under cover of night. With scouting parties far ahead and behind, keeping watch for the enemy. It was slow going. Each time a robot sighting was reported, the convoy was forced to pull the vehicles off the road using any cover they could find. Keeping the animals quiet was a challenge in and of itself.

"That has got to be the most ridiculous idea I've ever heard!" the president of Guatemala shouted. Others around her, nodded in agreement.

General Ford led the strategy meeting, flanked by Grant and Dr. Giggs. "Noted. Now please shut it."

Giggs jumped in before it could devolve into an argument. "The machines are behaving exactly like a hive mind, which tells us that they're coordinating their global attacks through digital signals. These signals must be originating from somewhere, and the hijacked space station is the most logical option."

The Japanese delegate spoke up. "Alright, suppose your message even got through, which, at this point we have no way of knowing. How do you know they'll come?"

Ford broke in, "There's not a doubt in my mind. This is the most stubborn, dedicated person I've ever known."

Not to be left out, the president of the United States, added his two cents. "Fine, assume the message was received. But how are we supposed to get a team up to the space station? It's not like walking around the corner to the convenience store. Heck, walking around the corner isn't like walking around the corner anymore."

The general nodded to his son for his part.

Grant cleared his throat, "I know how this all sounds, but we taught the machines everything we know, in hopes that they would go farther and end up teaching us. Unfortunately, it worked. They know exactly how we think. It's just another algorithm to them. So, the more ridiculous the plan, the higher probability we have of it working. In the meantime, all the robots seem to be communicating with each other all across the globe, which means there must be some sort of central hub or network down here on the surface. We need to find that and hit it at the same time we attack the station."

"Again, assuming your message got through." Someone shouted from the back.

The general kept his tone of voice even. "Like you said, travel is a bit tricky these days, but they'll be here."

"Why don't I feel any better about our situation?" Jackson asked. Hands on their heads, he and Daniel walked through the forest, flanked by the apes.

"If they wanted us dead, we would be already. They knew the difference and protected us from the robots, dad. At the very best, the robots would have captured us and kept us as prisoners."

Jackson looked all around him at the apes, who were clearly marching them somewhere specific. "Forgive me, kiddo. I'm not seeing much of a difference here."

After winding their way through the woods for a few miles, they came upon an old dirt road. Teetering on a ditch along the side were two trucks, covered in camo netting and some branches. They seemed to be abandoned. Beyond the road and back among the thick foliage was an encampment.

Dozens more primates were going about the business of gathering water, sorting supplies and making sure weapons were cleaned and loaded. Daniel was amazed at how efficiently they moved and worked.

The gorilla who led those guarding Daniel and Jackson, held up a closed fist and they all stopped. Unarmed and surrounded, Jackson took his son's hand, knowing there was no chance of escape.

"Hercules!" The voice which came from behind them, belonged to a woman. They turned to see Dr. Jessica Goodwin, the primatologist, emerge from the thick brush. She made several hand signals to the gorilla who nodded to his squad. They all lowered their weapons.

She walked right up to the hulking ape and looked directly in his eyes. They stood inches apart for a moment before she threw her arms around him, hugging tightly. Hercules, the gorilla playfully grunted. "Such a good boy!", she said. "You found survivors. I'm so proud of you". She let go of him and made some more hand signals, pointing to a barrel of apples. "Go ahead, eat something, all of you. Good job, you guys. Good job".

As the squad of apes moved off, the doctor approached Daniel and Jackson. "Heads up", she said, just before an apple bounced off Daniel's head.

One of the apes, a chimpanzee laughed. "That'd be Bella. I think she likes you, kid." Dr. Goodwin caught the next one before it could hit Jackson.

"So... um... Who exactly are you? What's with the apes? How did you get here? How did you find us? Are we your prisoners? What's going on?" Jackson asked.

She laughed. "We'll get to all of that. Take a minute, relax and catch your breath. You're safe now. If you're hungry, please help yourselves. If you can wait a bit, Edward is down by the river trying to teach some of the others to fish."

"So, what IS the deal with the apes?" Daniel asked. Looking around, he was amazed at how they worked as a cohesive team. Dr. Goodwin followed his eyes.

"They're my family. I've raised most of them since they were born."

"I was always more of a dog guy," Jackson chimed in.

Dr. Goodwin sat beside the fire with her unconventional platoon and told the newly found survivors how all of this came to be.

"Before all of this, I was the head of a sanctuary in San Diego. A lot of them are the children and grandchildren of apes trained for the space program. When the program got shut down, my.... Well, the head of N.S.E.P. sent them to me. Sort of retirement."

Daniel watched as Dr. Jepson patiently tried to teach a pair of chimpanzees how to clean the fish they had caught. The apes seemed far more interested in wrestling with each other.

"Those are the twins. Astro and Snot. Their grandfather was Berto, the first ape they tried to send into space. Nobody even knew his mate was pregnant until after the... Anyway, Astro would have made a heck of an astronaut and Snot is about the most loyal animal I've ever encountered."

115

"You met Bella earlier. She's pretty much the head of security, but don't say that around Hercules. He likes to think of himself as the alpha."

Jackson nodded towards a much older ape sitting on the hood of the truck. "And him?"

"That would be Darwin. He has the distinction of being the first one to survive space travel. He was never the same after that and he's too old to fight anymore. But the others look up to him and he likes to be useful. So, we put him on lookout. Your turn. What about you two? Are there others?"

Daniel and his dad shared a look. Jackson was still not completely sold on trusting this group, but Daniel was ready. After all, these apes had saved him twice now. Jackson probably couldn't have stopped him if he wanted to.

"We've been living in the woods since this started. We move around a lot, but try to stay close enough to the city, so we can scavenge food and whatever else we need. There were others, but the robots attacked and we got separated from them just before you showed up. I don't know how many were taken and how many escaped."

"Do you just stay close to this city, or do you travel from one to the next?" Goodwin asked.

"Just this one. This was our hometown," Daniel answered. "Most of us had lost someone here, and I guess we've all held out hope that somehow we'd find them or they'd come back. I know it's stupid and we'll probably never see them again. My mom was taken when I was little."

And that was all he wanted to say on the subject. "You know, I've seen you guys before. Well, not you and the human guy, but the apes. We were trapped in the city, and you were fighting the robots. That's how we got out of there. Is that what you guys do? Like rebels or something?"

"Not exactly. Not by choice, anyway. We're traveling to meet some people, and along the way, like you, we sometimes have to scavenge. We try to avoid the robots as much as possible."

"What people?", Jackson spoke up. "How did you communicate with them? Who are they? Other survivors? How many?"

From behind them, Jepson answered. "Slow down there. We shouldn't really say too much until we know each other a little better."

"That's a great idea!", Dr. Goodwin shouted. "Why don't you come with us?"

All three others responded in unison, "Wait, what?"

Dr. Jepson was shaking his head, "I don't think that's a good idea. We can't just bring strangers…"

"Not strangers, survivors!" she interrupted. "They need us. We can't just leave them out here. Besides, from a scientific perspective, they've observed the robots in the wild in a way that none of us have. So, we need them too."

"Whoa, hang on a second!" Jackson shouted. We were doing just fine out here on our own."

"Have we, though?" Daniel chimed in. "They've saved our butts twice now, in a few days."

"We've avoided being the robots' prisoners for years. I'm not about to blindly follow you or voluntarily let my son become yours." Jackson's voice was beginning to rise."

"Jackson's right", said Jepson.

"He's wrong!" Snapped both Daniel and Dr. Goodwin, simultaneously. They shared a look and a stubborn smile.

"I am taking my apes and whoever else here wants to join us. We're leaving in an hour and that's that." She gave Daniel a sly nod and wink.

"Wait, YOUR apes?" Dr. Jepson asked. "What about me?"

"I have paperwork from the government that says they're mine." She reminded him.

"You mean the government from before the world ended?" He asked. "I'm not sure that applies anymore."

"And yet, they reached out and asked me and MY apes for help. Time to start packing up and head out," she said, leaving him speechless. "One hour, all aboard who's coming aboard." And she walked off.

Daniel looked into his father's eyes before wordlessly following Dr. Goodwin. Jepson and Jackson just stared at each other awkwardly.

"Unfortunately, getting to space is probably the easy part," General Ford said. "And by easy, what I really mean is that it's just marginally less impossible. The most feasible course seems to be stealing one of the old Saturn rockets on display down in Florida. They're outdated and not connected to any networks. We don't know what shape they're currently in, so we're going to send a team, led by Dr. Giggs for a recon mission. With any luck, we should be able to simply fuel one up and go."

The Chinese president chimed in, "Those rockets have been sitting idle for decades!"

"Yes, but in a museum environment at the continually functional Space Program hub. Theoretically maintained for display. Again, Dr. Giggs and his team will check it out. Any small repairs or wires and hoses that may have rotted over time can hopefully be replaced with parts already on site."

"And how do you propose to fix, fuel and launch a massive rocket without being seen by the robots?" asked the Russian leader. "They're everywhere and as you say, it is still a functioning base. Surely there are active networks they are monitoring."

Ford turned the floor over to Dr. Giggs. "Uh, yes. Well, that's the more difficult part. We'll need to send a second team to disrupt, if not destroy the satellite signal so they can't see us. We have some intel that indicates the signal is received and disbursed from New Mexico. There may be others around the world, but this seems to be at least the center for this part of the globe."

Somebody in back shouted, "And where does this intel come from? How did you get it?"

"For now, I think that's best left classified. But I can assure you, my source is reliable."

Very politely, the Canadian Prime Minister raised his hand. "Excuse me? Um… Sorry to interrupt. But even if the intel is good and we're able to pull off all of these things, most, if not all of our militaries have been decimated. The only astronauts qualified for this insanity are already up there on the space station, and even they may be dead by now. Who is supposed to pilot this mission?"

<u>ROLLING THUNDER DRIVE-IN MOVIE THEATRE</u>

Dr. Goodwin drove the first of the two horse drawn trucks with Jackson and Daniel sitting beside her up front. Hercules was cramped in the back seat, annoyed by Astro and Snot. Dr. Jepson drove the other with Bella riding shotgun. Both trucks were packed with the rest of the apes. They pulled up to the locked gate of the run-down theater and waited.

After sitting there for what seemed like forever, Daniel asked, "Are you sure your friends made it?"

"They're here, she answered."

He and Jackson shared a look before adding, "Should you maybe honk the horn or something? Maybe they don't know we're here."

"They know", she replied. "Just do me a favor. Don't freak out."

And before they could even ask what she meant, they were surrounded by heavily armed Secret Service agents in camo and ghillie suits.

If one didn't know where to look for it, the massive freight elevator would never be found. The agents led Dr. Goodwin and company down at gunpoint. Maybe the elevator was just slow, but given the time that passed since they entered, it was more likely that they were a mile or so below ground. The hydraulic piston finally stopped and the door slid open. The Commanding Officer signaled the human passengers off. One of the agents made the mistake of moving between Dr. Goodwin and the apes. She found herself inches away and looking up into the angry face of Hercules. At his shoulder and ready to brawl, were Bella and several of the others. It was fast becoming a stand-off.

Trying to diffuse the situation, the Commander spoke up. "Doctor, I promise your animals…"

"My family," she cut him off.

With a sigh, the Commander continued. "I promise they'll be fine. There are a lot of delegates in the War-Room and I think it would be less distracting if they talk to you before they're introduced to the… Your family. We have an entire level allocated for you down below and when you're done in the War-Room, we can discuss getting you anything you might need. Now please." And he gestured to the door.

"Jessica," Dr. Jepson spoke up, "It's fine. We'll go with them and get settled. I'm not all that anxious to see the general anyway. You go talk to them. Daniel and Jackson will come with me. We'll be fine."

Without ever taking her eyes off the commanders, she signed to Hercules and Bella. "Stand down". And then out loud to the agents, "Lead the way."

As the lift gate began closing behind them, Daniel suddenly darted out. Neither his father nor the agents could stop him in time. The gate locked in place and the lift began to lower.

"I'm going with her! I've never seen a War-Room. I don't even know what that is. But I have to see it."

Jackson tried to object, but Dr. Goodwin said. "It's fine. C'mon Daniel."

The agent wasn't kidding. But you already knew that since you're almost a hundred pages in. The room was packed and a bit of a cacophony. World leaders were working with aides to send telegraphs to their home countries, engineers led by Dr. Giggs were pouring over paper blueprints and plans for rockets.

Dr. Goodwin was led through the throngs towards a work station where the general was briefing his son and a small special-ops team on the layout of the satellite array station in New Mexico. She stiffened when she saw them, took a deep breath and put on her game face.

Grant spotted her and gently tugged on his father's sleeve like a child. The general looked up and his words trailed off as she and Daniel approached. "Hello, Grant, hello, Sturgess."

Running to her, Grant pulled Dr. Goodwin into a big hug. "Hi, Mom", he said, surprising everyone… Well, almost everyone.

"It seems our apes are evolving", the general said, gesturing towards Daniel.

"*My* apes", she replied. "You gave them up when the government shut down the program. I have the paperwork. This is Daniel Todd. He and his father are survivors we met on the road."

"I'm not entirely sure any paperwork holds up in this world anymore," He said.

"Not the first time I've heard that" She Replied.

With a scowl, General Ford eyeballed the boy. "Well, I definitely don't think this room is any place for a civilian, let alone a civilian child."

Daniel stood his ground, returning the general's stink-eye in kind.

"Are you two really going to do this now?" Grant interrupted. "Can we maybe table the resentment until after the world is saved?"

Dr. Goodwin grinned at her son. "I missed you, Grant." And then turned back to the general, "This kid has lived most of his life on street level, fighting and surviving the machines. I'm willing to bet nobody else in this room has as much experience as him. He stays. Who knows, maybe you warriors will learn something."

*****

Back in the lift, heading down to the apes, Daniel asked, "So, how does all of this work?"

"All of what?" Grant replied.

"I saw all those messaging machines and TV screens. Not to mention, the lights are on and we're riding in an elevator. You're getting power from somewhere. How do the robots not find you?"

Grant was impressed. "Pretty observant, kid. Mostly solar. We also have windmills as backup. Nothing networked by computer. The solar panels are about six-hundred miles away from here and the windmills a bit further in the opposite direction. All the cabling is buried a couple of miles underground. And the telegraphs are connected by good old-fashioned telephone lines from long before the world started using fiber-optics. Again, buried deep. It's risky, but the robots haven't found them yet and hopefully they won't before we stop them."

The elevator opened into the largest chamber Daniel had ever seen. Concrete walls stretched off into the darkness. Vehicles, including the trucks they arrived in, were parked along the walls. Beyond that were the stables of horses and oxen whose job it was to pull them.

Daniel spotted his dad and ran to him, excited to tell him what he had seen. He waved Grant to follow so he could introduce them.

The general and Dr. Goodwin stepped off the elevator, met by agents. "Ma'am, as promised, everyone is safe and sound. This will be your home for the time being, so please just make a list of anything you need and we'll accommodate you in any way we can."

"Yeah, yeah, yeah," Ford grunted. "Later. Just let us go see the apes."

124

"Yes, Sir.   Over there, Sir," the agent in charge replied, pointing.

And that's when the general spotted Dr. Jepson. "You've got to be kidding me. What's HE doing here?"

"Be nice, Sturgess." She said, gently elbowing him in the ribs. "Besides me, he's been more responsible for raising and training them than anyone."

"The man's an idiot."

"He's incredibly kind and compassionate. The apes love him. More importantly, they trust him."

"So, what are you two? Like a…. You know, a…"

She couldn't help but chuckle. "A couple? That's none of your business." Then seeing what looked a little bit like jealousy in the general's eyes, she softened. "After the program was terminated, he just wanted to still be around them."

"Whatever. Let's see what we're working with, shall we," He nodded to the head agent who signaled the entire team. They headed to the elevator. "One level down is an obstacle course. Have you taught them how to play Capture the Flag? I'll give you five minutes to get your team ready."

Dr. Goodwin grinned. "We only need three. Oh, and tell your team they may want to wear pads."

<u>A.G.D.A. COMBAT TRAINING LEVEL (2 MINUTES, 53 SECONDS LATER)</u>

The training course was vast. Littered with dirt hills, concrete K-rail barriers and sandbag bunkers. Camouflage netting hung from the rafters and trucks were parked randomly throughout.

Just below the rafters, gallery windows lining the top of the level were cramped with the anxious faces as Grant, Daniel, Jackson and all the delegates, looked down upon the obstacle course some twenty feet below.

The apes faced off against the soldiers. Both teams were armed with paintball guns. General Ford and the two doctors stood between them.

"While your monkeys have been lounging in their sanctuary, my troops have trained on this course every day since the war began." The general lectured. "These men and women represent some of the finest soldiers I've ever seen, and they've been aching for some competition. I have to warn you; my soldiers absolutely will not take it easy on your pets. So, while I'm not expecting any miracles, I at least hope you can show me something I can use."

Just then, a yellow paintball exploded on the general's chest. Most of the apes laughed while Bella looked away, avoiding eye contact with the humans. Dr. Jepson did his best (and failed) not to laugh. The general simply smacked him upside the head.

"I think that means my team is ready," Dr. Goodwin said with a grin as she handed Ford a bandana to clean off the paint.

"Fine. First team to capture five enemy flags, wins."

Most of the human soldiers hunkered down behind obstacles with three stationed back-to-back, forming a perimeter around the flag. They were broken into small, disciplined squads, awaiting the signal to fan out and charge from several directions. The apes chattered and grunted loudly from seemingly random positions at their end with none near their flag.

"On my count," shouted the general. "Three... Two... One!" And he blasted an air horn.

The soldiers sprang up. Precise, well-trained movements, they began to charge. But before they gained even a few yards, a loud buzzer sounded from the speakers. Everybody froze.

The three soldiers standing guard looked around, oblivious to Snot, the chimp, behind them. He dangled upside down as his twin, Astro, held his ankles while hanging from the rafters.

Snot snatched the flag in his paw and Astro lifted him up before guards had even noticed it was gone.

Dr. Goodwin held up a single finger, making sure the general knew they had one point.

"That's not fair!" He told her. "How are my men supposed to..."

"They're not," she cut him off. "That's kind of exactly why you brought us here. One, nothing, us."

Up in the gallery, the delegates didn't know how to react. Daniel high-fived Jackson and gave Dr. Goodwin a thumbs up. She returned it with a wink.

The teams reset at their respective ends of the course. This time the soldiers guarding the flag were ready. Six of them now, all back to back around the flag, watching the rafters. The apes were all spread out. They seemed to be laughing at their human counterparts.

The air horn blasted again, and the humans charged. So did the apes, only they charged their own flag. Bella grabbed it and handed it off to Hercules, the gorilla. Hercules threw it up to a small capuchin monkey climbing one of the cargo nets. It was chaos.

The humans tried to follow it, firing at and missing the apes as they passed the flag between them. The apes' speed was dizzying and confused the soldiers, which was exactly the plan. Four more chimps crawled past the final bunker and splattered the six guards in yellow paint as they were busy looking up. They easily grabbed the flag. The buzzer sounded once more and the apes immediately put their own flag back.

"Way to go, guys!" Dr. Goodwin shouted to her apes, clapping her hands.

General Ford shouted at her, "This is Capture the Flag, not Keep Away."

"Consider it defense if it makes you feel better. And seeing how we're two points up and you're six men down, seems like it worked."

Above, Grant couldn't hear what his parents were saying, but he could easily tell that she was getting to him. *Just like old times*, he thought, grinning.

The general huddled up his troops around him. "Listen, morons. I wanted to show that the apes were viable but this is embarrassing. You're never going to get that flag unless you take out those apes. Just plant your feet and clear that field! Do not stop firing until you get every last one of them"

"Hey," Jepson taunted from the sideline. "Are there time-outs in war? You guys need a water break?"

Ford was fuming. He scolded his team, "Just get it done!" And as he sprinted from the course, he blew the horn once again.

The soldiers immediately opened fire on the apes and it seemed to work as the apes scattered using anything they could to climb out of the way. As they scrambled up the nets, into the rafters, clung to the hanging lights above, the soldiers relentlessly fired at them.

The delegates flinched as the humans' red paint pinged and splattered the gallery windows, obscuring their view. The bulbs in the hanging lights shattered from paintball impact. The course was growing darker and darker as the apes swung and climbed as fast as they could. They kept moving until the last light was shot out.

Once it was pitch black in the room, there was a brief moment of silence before the sound of paintball air rifles started up again. This time it was short. And then it just stopped all together.

When the emergency lights came on, the human soldiers were covered from head to toe in yellow paint. Bella casually strolled over to the flag and pulled it from its base, sounding the buzzer. She cheerfully carried it over and laid it at the general's feet before offering him an exaggerated salute.

And then she shot him again.

"Bella!" Dr. Goodwin scolded her out loud while in sign language telling her, "You're my hero". She then turned back to Ford, "Looks like we win."

The general scoffed, "We're playing to five. This only makes three. Spending so much time with them, have you forgotten how to count?"

"You can't fight a war without an army and you're all out of soldiers. Weird, I can't see any paint on any of my team." She again handed him her bandana. "Here. Something I know you can use."

She and Jepson walked off the course to join their team, offering Hercules a fist-bump as they passed.

The general called after them, "You and your team, report to the psychological and behavioral testing level in twenty minutes."

Dr. Goodwin stopped in her tracks. "You've got to be kidding me! We just fought our way across the country and still kicked your soldiers' butts. We need to rest, eat something."

"Like your boyfriend said," Ford grinned slyly. "No time-outs in war. Twenty minutes."

<u>A.G.D.A. BEHAVIORAL TESTING LEVEL</u>

Another large chamber with windows lining the upper walls for observers. Stark white tile walls with overly bright, sterile fluorescent lighting. This one was far more like a laboratory than the others.

The apes were being made to entertain their diplomatic audience by doing all manner of behavioral tests and puzzles, and they seemed none too happy about it. Most were solving pattern problems and putting blocks through matching holes. Astro and Snot were playing with the rings of a Hanoi tower, wearing them like jewelry.

"Really?", Darwin signed to Dr. Jepson. "Don't they know I've been doing these since I was a child?" and he shoved the tangram pieces away.

"Just play along," Jepson signed back.

Whenever somebody tried to get near Hercules, he just grunted and beat his chest to chase them off. Then he would go back to reading a book.

"Why does he pretend to read?" an attendant asked.

"Oh, he's not pretending. Once we taught them to sign, that led to teaching them the alphabet and then to equating text to words. They're not reading quantum physics or anything, but most of them can do it with varying degrees of real comprehension."

Bella, on the other hand didn't care. She took the Rubik's cube they handed her and easily solved it in under a minute. She had always loved showing humans that she was smarter than them. The attendant inspected it, impressed. But Bella grabbed it back and scrambled it again. She then pushed it across the table.

Dr. Goodwin laughed and told the attendant, "She wants to see if you can do it."

"Look, I know what these apes are capable of. I know how well you've taught them," General Ford told her. "But we need to convince these people that this is a viable option. Just put on the show for ten more minutes, and I promise they'll get all the food and rest they need. You have to remember how crazy this must sound to these people."

And that set her off. "Seriously? How crazy DOES it sound to them? As crazy, maybe, as robots taking over the world? By the way, aren't some of these people the ones we have to thank for that in the first place? And do they not remember trying to train apes to be astronauts, once upon a time?"

"First of all, the astronaut program was a failure. And second, one of those people you have to thank for this, happens to be our son. You'd remember that if you hadn't been hiding in the incredibly well-equipped sanctuary which by the way, I set up for you!"

"Hey, I did more than keep up my end of the bargain! I've taught them far more than the military ever imagined! Far better than you ever could. Y'know? Funny how you seem to be the common denominator in all this. So, this is what? Your chance at redemption?"

"This isn't about me, it's not about you, it's a chance to save the world! Can you please just put aside all that other crap and help?"

She looked up and saw Daniel talking with Grant. "Fine. They'll do the parlor tricks. When we're done, you can brief me on the mission and we'll get to work. They'll be much more agreeable once we can get to the real training. And I promise, all your friends will be super-impressed."

A.G.D.A COMPOUND – BARRACKS LEVEL

It had been a long time since Daniel and Jackson had eaten so well, let alone slept in beds. Sure, they were simple metal cots, but they had mattresses and clean blankets. Jackson would have felt much guiltier about soaking in the hot shower, but as others pointed out, robots can't smell – humans can.

They were issued clean military fatigues, but due to his size, Daniel had to wear a flight suit made for the apes. He felt silly in it - even once he was sure that there was no hole cut into the seat for a tail - but he was grateful. Especially when he considered that he couldn't remember the last time he was someplace that actually had electricity.

They were examined by doctors and despite how they had been living for several years, they checked out just fine.

Wandering the level designated to them and the apes, Daniel wondered where Goodwin, Jepson and the lead apes were. He tried to get on the elevator only to be stopped by a guard. "Sorry Kid, they're all in a briefing. It's classified. I'm under orders, you and your father need to stay here." Daniel skulked off, back to his bunk area and pulled out his journal.

I can't stop thinking about all the others we left behind. Hopefully they were able to get away and hide. I keep wondering what the robots do with the people they catch. I've seen them get grabbed and dragged off, but what do they do with them? Could they still be alive? If so, could mom still be alive? I honestly don't know which would be worse. Maybe we can somehow find a way to save them, but if not.... Best not to even think about it now.

Dr. Goodwin, Dr. Jepson and their apes are amazing. For the first time, I feel like maybe we can end this war. But like dad always says, if I want to help anybody, I have to stay alive. I'm sure he won't like it but there's no way I'm not going on whatever this mission is. Now, all I have to do is survive. How hard can that be? I've done it most of my life.

That was the heading on the map projected up on the screen. It showed the sixteen-hundred-acre area comprised of lush jungle, rocky hills and arid plains. There were man-made lakes, ponds and waterfalls scattered throughout. Closer to the center were the lab, medical center and educational facilities.

Bella, Hercules and Darwin sat at the center of the dais affront the War-Room, flanked on either side by Dr.'s Goodwin and Jepson. The rest of the seats were occupied by Grant Ford, Dr. Stanley Giggs and finally General Sturgess Ford.

"At our facility, we have done all we can in order for these amazing animals to continue being just that." The screen changed, now showing apes pulling fruit from trees and rooting for grubs in the soil. "I believe that – with all due respect – the failure of the space program was in trying to modify their behavior to more human patterns. The majority of our apes were born at the reserve and have never lived in the wild, but none of them were raised by humans. Every one of them is raised by the apes themselves on our property. Apes are highly intelligent, instinctive creatures. They are remarkable mimics, but we tend to forget that our human behaviors are counterintuitive to them. Their priorities are simply different from ours."

The delegate from Japan raised his hand, "But the things we saw them do with our own eyes: The war games, the problem-solving exercises? Surely that's not instinctive behavior. You had to have trained them to accomplish those things."

"Yes and no," Goodwin answered. "The first apes that came to us had spent time with humans. The military, to be precise. We had taken them from their homes, strapped them into machines, shoved them into tin cans and shot them into orbit. They were afraid of us. Performing those tasks were nothing more than acts of self-preservation. They did as they were told, for fear of consequence."

The monitor changed to show old security footage of the first-generation apes being released into the preserve. "After we introduced them to the habitat, we simply left them alone. We designed this place to be familiar to the surroundings we had originally taken them from. Of course, the environment was more controlled than the wild, but we did all we could to keep from stepping in. The first year was tough, as they acclimated to their surroundings. But it was also in that first year, as we simply observed them, that we saw the first amazing steps to the apes here with us today."

The delegates were shown more footage of a small monkey at the top of a tall tree, dropping the fruit it picked down to a gorilla down on the ground. "Apes and monkeys tend to be very territorial creatures. Maybe it was their time in the program together or the shock of suddenly being on their own again, but we saw interspecies cooperation. That cooperation quickly grew into an incredibly protective, supportive and most importantly, singular community."

"But that doesn't explain how you were able to train them," came another voice from the back.

Jepson smiled at Dr. Goodwin. He knew she had been baiting the delegates to just this question. She returned his look before again changing the video monitor. The image showed her slowly and carefully approaching a cluster of mixed apes. She kept her head down and hands exposed in a non-threatening manner. The apes shrieked, jumped up and down and pounded their chests to establish dominance. She paused the video just after showing her walking directly into the middle and kneeling submissively.

"I didn't train them. I started by letting them train me." Her statement was met by a series of grumbles from the audience. "As I said, they were afraid of humans. They certainly didn't trust us. Once I saw that they had become confident enough on their own, I began integrating myself into their community by doing as they did. I let them teach me their ways. Once I had earned their trust, I started introducing members of our staff into the community."

"We were there for the births of their children, the loss of elder family members, everything. But we did it all on their terms. We weren't their masters, we were just part of the family. Over time, their teaching me, evolved into a sharing of thoughts. Apes are incredibly curious animals. They couldn't get enough of learning new things. As long as it was on their own terms. The biggest test came when we reintroduced Dr. Jepson, here. He had been their primary trainer at N.S.E.P for a time and we feared that they would remember and associate him with that difficult time in their lives."

She scrolled through a series of photos of Jepson with the apes. In several of them, he was covered in bruises, scratches and bite marks. In one, he was even in a cast. "It's a credit to his patience, commitment and in fact, his love for the apes, that we've gotten to where we are now." The video continued cycling through a slideshow of the apes learning things like sign language, chess, and eventually even training in flight simulators. "We're incredibly lucky to have him."

Don't think for a moment that she hadn't done it on purpose or that she didn't notice the reaction. General Ford rolled his eyes. And then she added, "But of course, we couldn't have accomplished any of this without the funding and equipment generously arranged by General Sturgess Ford." He was startled by this, and when he met her eye, she gave a quick wink and smile.

"You said it yourselves. You've seen with your own eyes what these apes are capable of. And it's because of these two great men that we've been able to continue the program, which will hopefully now save mankind in our hour of need. So, let's get to it."

Even if all the delegates weren't convinced, none of them had a better plan. And thus, the mission was officially greenlit.

The apes were given a few days to rest up and get acclimated to their new surroundings. They still didn't trust the soldiers or bureaucrats, so they mostly stuck together on their level. They and the doctors had definitely taken a liking to Daniel, essentially making him part of the tribe.

Daniel eagerly involved himself in everything they did. He trained with them, ate with them and played with them.

Grant Ford liked him as well. He began teaching Daniel about engineering and computers. Of course, they couldn't actually use computers, but through schematics and text books, at least he could give a theoretical base. The kid seemed to impressively soak up the information like a sponge. But Daniel was never happier than when running the obstacle course with the apes. He was especially close with Bella and Hercules who had formed a sort of competition for his attention.

Jackson felt increasingly helpless among the scientists, the troops and the delegates. It wasn't jealousy so much as a desire to be useful. Before falling in with this lot, he was the leader of their group of survivors. Now instead, he just felt as if he was constantly getting in the way. He grew more and more concerned for his son. Not only did he simply want to keep Daniel safe, but he watched as the boy grew more and more attached to the apes and their handlers. Inevitably Daniel would want to go on whatever crazy mission this was and there was no way Jackson would allow it. Absolutely no way. He had been through so much already and Jackson couldn't bear the thought of him getting his hopes up for such a long shot of success.

*****

Giggs packed up some gear, including a metal security briefcase and a portable telegraph machine. Along with a small team of mechanics and soldiers he was going to head down the coast by boat to scout the Space Center.

General Ford had supplied him with a detailed map of the N.S.E.P. campus as well as schematics for all of the spacecraft housed there. The team was briefed on security measures - allowing for the probability that the robots had upgraded, changed or added to them. They were shown how to fuel the rockets.

They would leave under cover of night, hopefully allowing them to go unseen as the boat left port. Even if they were lucky and avoided all enemy contact, it would take several days to travel down the coast. They were mandated to travel by sail, only using the motors for emergencies.

Best case scenario, if all went well with the recon excursion, they could be mission ready and on the move in three weeks. However, the current projections put them conservatively at six weeks out.

Given the circumstances, engineers did what they could to cobble together serviceable flight simulators, replicas of the space station and the rockets.

The primitive spacecraft's lack of reliance on computers made them easier to recreate here in the training center, but it also made them much harder to fly on an actual mission with any degree of accuracy.

Fortunately, several of the delegates from around the world were former astronauts themselves. From those, they were able to recruit a team of four who were still physically fit and capable enough to pilot the ship.

The final crew was comprised of Sergei Andreyev from Russia, Li Wei Liu, a medic from China, Steve Johnston and Mike Rodgers form the United States. They would train and join six of the apes on the trip to space, along with one of the animal handlers. The six apes would be chosen based on their specific skills and appraisals during the training.

The bulk of the apes would join a human contingent on a mission to shut down communications at the New Mexico satellite array. Once again, the agents and soldiers made their appraisals during training in order to better form a battle strategy.

Integrating the humans and apes proved difficult. Clearly, Dr. Goodwin's lecture on gaining trust went mostly unheard as General Ford and his men kept on trying to force the apes into human patterns and behaviors.

"Why don't you just teach them to sign, so they can talk to each other?" The entire level fell silent when Daniel asked.

"I thought they already knew sign language," The general dismissed.

Dr. Goodwin laughed. "Pretty sure he was talking about your men."

SOMEWHERE OFF THE EAST COAST OF THE UNITED STATES

When we think of sail boats, we tend to picture luxurious yachts with people sipping champagne on deck. Tall white sails billowing on bright summer days.

That's not remotely what this was.

Three nights into their voyage, the crew was fighting against the cold bitter weather three miles off the coast. The boat was an armored catamaran, painted flat black with no markings. Even the sail was dark material, matching the color of the waters themselves. The weight of the armor made it hard to steer in the rough seas. Troops manned the weapons bolted to the deck. They had been lucky so far, having no sightings, let alone contact with the enemy. Maybe the weather had been a blessing in that sense. The robots knew us, and hopefully thought people were smarter than trying to navigate in these conditions.

Below deck, Dr. Stanley Giggs tried to occupy himself by checking to make sure his gear was properly stowed. In this weather, Giggs didn't want his equipment tossed around much like his cookies had… repeatedly. He figured he would have gotten used to the motion by now, and the seasickness would have passed, but… nope. Not even a little. Giggs wretched again, and it was for this reason—the smell specifically—that none of the soldiers complained about getting guard duty on deck.

<u>A.G.D.A. BEHAVIORAL TESTING LEVEL</u>

The room was set up like a classroom. Daniel was front and center, surrounded by soldiers. The general stood begrudgingly in the back, occasionally being elbowed in the ribs by Grant when he thought his dad wasn't paying attention to the lesson.

Up at the front of the class, Darwin gave an entirely silent speech. His gestures weren't fast, but deliberate. He had been warned by Dr. Goodwin that he had to treat these soldiers like children or they wouldn't understand.

When he was done, Dr. Goodwin asked, "So, can anybody tell me what he was saying?" She was met by a roomful of blank stares, shoulder shrugs and people avoiding eye contact.

Seeing this, Daniel sheepishly raised his hand. She asked him to stand. He did, self-consciously and answered. "I think he was reciting the lyrics from 'Star Crossed' by the Bitter Pills. Released in nineteen-seventy-three on Atomic Records."

"Impressive. How did you know?" The Dr. asked. Most of the soldiers' jaws dropped. Some threw their arms up in frustration. The general shook his head.

"I'm kind of a music buff. I got it from my mom. That was a favorite of hers."

Goodwin smiled at him and then signed Daniel's answer to Darwin, who started clapping his hands. "He's very impressed. But what I meant was, how did you recognize it? Do you know how to sign?"

Daniel shook his head, "Not really. But since I met you guys, I've just sorta watched them. I was able to pick out a few words here and there, and y'know, recognized the song."

"Clever kid," Grant said. And that was too much for his dad. General Ford stormed up to the front of the class. "Listen up! We're on a clock here, people. The feral kid here...," and looked at Daniel. "Sorry kid, no offense. If he can figure it out, you should be able to as well. I don't want to have to choose between 'Independence Day' and 'Planet of the Apes!' Now get it together, people!"

Daniel leaned over and muttered something to the soldier next to him. The general didn't like the distraction. "You have something to add?"

"I was just asking what you meant by 'Planet of the Apes' and the other thing you said."

"It's a movie. They're both movies. What's the matter with you?"

"I've never seen a movie. I was too young, before all of this."

Again, Goodwin cut in. "Alright, alright. Look, let's just try it again. Now you know what he's saying, just try to follow along. All of the signs are right there on the white board." As she signed to Darwin, she also spoke out loud. "Go ahead, Darwin. Slower this time."

A.G.D.A. COMPOUND – N.S.E.P. TRAINING LEVEL

In the biggest swimming pool, you've ever imagined, the engineers built a full-size replica of the space station to simulate zero-gravity. The first hurdle was getting the apes to actually go in - as it's a well-known fact that apes don't like water.

Daniel was sulking since the astronauts wouldn't let him train to go into space. He almost petulantly ignored everything going on around him. Instead, he wrote in his journal:

It's just not fair! I've proved I'm every bit as capable as the apes and smarter than probably most of the soldiers. But no! I'm "just a kid. It's too dangerous. Blah, blah, blah." I mean, I kind of get it but I've done and seen so much. As much as any of them have.

I like Doctors Jepson and Goodwin, but I would have thought that at least one of them would have been on my side. Sure, the general is a jerk and I can't even pretend that dad would have ever been okay with me going into space. But still... It's just not fair!

Jackson took a seat beside his son who immediately closed his journal. "You alright, pal?" Daniel barely even acknowledged his presence. "Look, believe it or not, I get it. But this is their job, not ours."

"Why not?" Daniel snapped. "This is our war too! We've been fighting it the whole time, protecting the people who depended on us! Don't we deserve a little payback? We lost so many; we lost Mom! Doesn't that mean anything?!"

"This isn't about payback!" Jackson lost his temper. "That's what you're not getting. That's why you're not ready to go up there to the space station! You think I don't miss your mother, that I don't wish I could go rescue her or the countless others the robots took? I hate to break it to you, kiddo, but we have no idea what they did with them. We have no reason to even believe that they could still be alive! The best I can do is keep you alive and to be honest, I feel like I'm failing at that! I... We've spent years looking out for other people. How's that worked out so far? Maybe it's time to let someone look out for us for a while. Forget it. We did our part. Why can't you just let them do theirs?"

"Because I'm not a quitter!" Daniel said as he stormed off, leaving his father feeling even worse than he already had.

*****

Maybe it was because Dr. Goodwin and Jepson suited up and got in the water. Maybe it was because they had actually begun to accept if not trust their human counterparts. But most likely, they did it because they didn't like being shown up by the humans.

Being as agile as apes are, they seemed to figure out pretty quickly how to move around in the water. And once they did, they were remarkably dexterous. After a while, some of them even started to enjoy it. To the point where it became difficult to get the twins, Astro and Snot, to stop fooling around and focus on the mission.

Bella was all business. Her movements were quick and efficient. The soldiers and astronauts quickly came not only to respect, but admire her abilities. Being just a bit smaller than an adult human, she was able to navigate with ease through the tubes which represented the passages of the space station.

Hercules, on the other hand, was another story entirely. More than once, he actually broke the station pieces. Partly due to his being so big, but mostly because he would get so frustrated and lose his temper. Sergei Andreyev finally had to ask Goodwin to get him out of the pool.

The team had decided to anchor the boat safely out at sea. Lowering the mast and using the dark blue sail as a tarp, they covered the craft, making it nearly invisible to the eye, or more importantly, the robots' cameras. As the sun dipped below the horizon, two men remained onboard while the rest paddled inflatable rafts to shore. It was much slower going, but also far less conspicuous.

There was a small cove lined with trees where they could pull the rafts ashore and stash them without being seen. It was out on the peninsula that housed the old launch gantry. They would have to go on foot for about a half-mile, to the main campus.

The soldiers kept careful watch as the mechanics offloaded their gear. Giggs had a moment of panic when he couldn't find his briefcase until he spotted one of the others holding it. "Um, I'll take that one if you don't mind." The mechanic shrugged and handed it over.

Captain Harold Stack suddenly held up a closed fist signaling all the others to freeze. He had spotted movement in the brush and looked through his scope, trying to see what it was. "Just a gator," he said.

"That's just perfect," one of the others muttered. "Clearly robots weren't enough of a threat."

"We're on their turf, so there's bound to be more. Just keep your eyes peeled. If we're lucky they'll distract any robots from us. Evans, take Johansen. Go scout ahead and report back what we're walking into. Dr. Giggs, you and your team check and prep your gear. Take only what's absolutely necessary. Be ready to move out in ten minutes."

"Take everything," Giggs told the mechanics. "We won't know what we'll need until I can put eyes on the situation. I need to know where the rocket is in conjunction to the fuel. I have to see what condition it's in and if it would even be possible to launch."

Exactly ten minutes later, the two soldiers returned. After a quick report to the commanding officer, Stack in turn, briefed the others. "The priority is to survey layout and security. If and ONLY if I say it's safe, you and your team can move forward with any repairs. Doctor Giggs, you're what we call 'mission critical', you stay tight on me. We don't know what's out there and my men may not be able to protect yours if they get lost or fall behind. Are we clear?" That last part obviously wasn't really a question, since he turned and walked off without waiting for the answer.

The half-mile walk was nothing to the soldiers, but to the mechanics it was arduous. Bogged down with equipment in the humidity and having to go so slowly.

A main cluster of buildings would provide cover as they moved across the campus. Inside the visitor's center, Giggs grabbed a pamphlet from the counter they hid behind. It was a map. Thank goodness for tourist attractions.

About a hundred yards beyond that loomed what was known as the Rocket Garden. A proud monument to spacecraft of the past. There were ten in all, from the very first rocket to break the atmosphere, all the way through Space Shuttle Program. Most of them stood upright, pointing to the heavens. Resting on a stand was a massive Saturn class Rocket. The display had it angled up at a forty-five-degree angle with its nose pointed East, towards the sunrise.

"There! That's the one," Giggs said. "Barring any major damage, that's our best chance to launch."

The Captain took a moment to look. "Wait, all the rockets out there, and you want to take the one lying on its side? You're kidding, right?

"Those others, aside from being much smaller – which would mean sending a smaller team up, are not standing on their own. This is Florida. Hurricane territory. They have to be bolted or welded in place somehow so they don't blow over. There are no gantries, so even if we did launch, there's no guiding structure for lift off."

"Exactly," Stack argued. "But that one is already laying down! We'd have to lift it upright first. On what planet does that make any sense at all?"

Exasperated, Giggs shook his head. "On a round planet, which most rational people would agree, Earth is.

Look at the stand it's on. It's angled upward, with a clear shot out over the ocean where the astronauts will simply need to maintain a straight path past the curvature of the Earth and through the atmosphere. That's not even physics, it's elementary geometry. Normally, this place would be inhabited, so the blast from a horizontal ignition would be a problem. But in the present circumstance, we don't need to worry about that. The wall from that building there may actually provide some pressure to the blast, giving the rocket additional thrust. Again, assuming the ship itself can be made launch-ready."

The Captain checked his watch, "We're about three hours from sun-up. I'm guessing your team will need more time than that. So, for now, my men will cover while you inspect the rocket and figure out what it will take to fix and fuel it. Johansen, find some covered high ground and keep watch. At first light, we leave the gear hidden here and come back after the sun goes down tonight."

A.G.D.A. TRAINING LEVEL

Apes, astronauts, soldiers and civilians alike stood in formation. General Ford faced them. "Okay, listen up. We need to be ready to move out at any minute. We've made our selections for the team going into space. Obviously our four astronauts will be going. With them will be Dr. Jepson and six of his apes. We're awaiting word from the recon team to determine any additional equipment or personnel that we need. This team will be escorted by a security detail consisting of both human and simian soldiers."

The general moved to a large map on the wall. "First, however, our other team will head out here," he said, pointing to the New Mexico desert. "The objective is to destroy the satellite array and disrupt the robots' communication network by any means necessary. Travel will be slow going for the obvious reasons. Our demolition specialist, Captain Lindt and his team will take out the dishes while Doctor Goodwin will lead the bulk of her ape… uh, I mean troops to combat any resistance they encounter. And let me be clear, we are anticipating heavy resistance. Time is a factor. This target is twice as far as the launch site, and being that our own communications system is janky at best, this team needs to move out immediately in order to line up with the launch team. Assuming, of course, that a launch is actually possible."

He looked out into the faces of all the men and apes and took a deep breath before continuing,

"Look. Full disclosure time. The odds of success on either front, are not in our favor. But all of you here in this room represent our best and only hope. You're all here because I believe you can do this. We can't lay out any specific battle plans because we don't know what we're facing. This is a 'Hail Mary' play. We're blindly marching into the impossible. Remember, the robots know how we think. They know our strategies. That's why doctor Goodwin and her team are here. They're unpredictable. So, I want all our human troops to adopt that same principle. Don't try to make them behave like humans. Follow their

149

lead, learn to behave like apes. Stay fluid, improvise and we
may just pull this lunacy off. Good luck to you all."

N.S.E.P. COMPOUND

The sun was beginning to set over the outskirts of the base. Most of the team was prepping their incursion to the Rocket Garden. Doctor Giggs had taken a seat in one of the rubber rafts. He was fiddling with whatever was in his open briefcase when Captain Stack startled him and he slammed the case shut.

"Little jittery, ain't ya' Doc?"

Giggs scowled, "I think jittery is an appropriate state, given the current situation. Don't you, Captain?"

"Fair enough. But now we're going to need you to put on your big-boy pants and knuckle up. We move out in ten minutes." And noticing how tightly Giggs was hugging the case, he added, "What've you got there?"

Giggs looked down at it and responded, "Nothing. I wouldn't expect you to understand. Ten minutes, you said? I'll be ready. Now, if you'll excuse me so I can collect myself."

The Captain nodded and studied Giggs' eyes as he asked, "You sure you're okay? Nothing you want to tell me?"

"Ten minutes," was all Giggs replied. The two just stared at each other for a long tense moment before the Captain walked off. Once Giggs was sure he was alone, he opened up the briefcase. Inside was an old brick of a laptop computer. He opened the lid and began typing.

The apes and soldiers finally seemed to be working well together. They loaded trucks and prepped the horses and oxen to pull them. Several of the humans had picked up sign language easily and were able to actually have conversations with the apes.

Doctor Goodwin stood with the space station team to say her goodbyes. As she signed to them, she couldn't shake the thought that she very likely would never see them again. Astro, Snot, Kong - the capuchin monkey, Conan – A baboon, Titus and Bella were clearly feeling the same way.

"I know the general's little pep-talk was less than encouraging, but I wouldn't have brought you here if I didn't believe in you or the mission. You can and will get it done. Doctor Edward will be with you. And you know he wouldn't go if he thought we couldn't win. Our tribe has grown much bigger now, so if you all work together, everything will be fine in the end. But no matter how this turns out, I couldn't be prouder of you all, and to be a part of this family." She was having a hard time fighting back the tears as she hugged each of the apes. To the human crew, her voice grew much sterner. "I meant it. You're all part of the tribe now. Keep each other safe." Finally, to Dr. Jepson, she asked, "You're sure you're up to this?"

"How could I not be? My whole life has been about two things, the Space Program and these apes. What could be a more poetic culmination than this? Besides, I wouldn't want Bella to think I'm a chicken." They shared a smile. "You be safe and take good care of the others. Your mission is every bit as dangerous as ours. Last one back buys dinner." And he gave her a hug.

Just then, General Ford cleared his throat. "Jepson. You and your team have two more days of training before you head out. I'd suggest you go use them wisely. Jessica, it's time for your squad to move out." She took one last look at them, nodded and walked off with the general towards the trucks.

Her team was already onboard and ready. Grant was there waiting with Jackson and Darwin. To Jackson she asked, "Where's Daniel? The apes were wanting to say goodbye."

Jackson shrugged, "This is just hard on him. I'm sure he's upset that I won't let him go with you."

She nodded her understanding while shaking his hand. "He's an amazing kid. You've done a great job raising him. Tell him I said so."

Grant gave her a big long hug. "Feels like you just got here. I wish you didn't have to go."

She pulled back to arms-length to look him squarely in the eye. "Me too, kiddo, but as someone recently told me. This isn't about me. We all have to do our parts. You take care of Darwin and the old guy while I'm gone."

Then finally, she turned to the general, "...And by the way? No."

Confused, he asked, "No? No, what? I didn't ask you anything."

She leaned in and kissed him on the cheek. "No, Jepson and I were never a couple."

He grinned at that and added, "Thought that was none of my business?"

She was already climbing aboard her truck, but called back over her shoulder, "We'll talk about it when I get back."

Sergeant Johansen was perched atop the Visitors' Center when he heard a rustling in the trees. It wasn't easy to see since the sun had gone down, but he was reasonably certain it must be the team returning. He checked his watch, quietly rolled to the side of the building and with his weapon slung across his shoulders, shimmied down the same drain pipe he used to get up.

He jumped the last several feet so as to intercept the others before they broke the tree line. Startled though they were, they stayed quiet. Johansen held up the closed fist signal to freeze and signaled them to get down and wait. He pointed to his watch and then out to the clearing between them and the rocket garden.

A pair of ten-foot-tall robots passed. They were obviously sentries on patrol. Their domed heads swiveling in search of intruders. Lieutenant Evans raised his weapon, but Johansen grabbed him by the wrist and shook his head. He signaled to just wait.

The robots kept moving on a pre-determined path. Think of those automatic vacuum cleaners, only giant and with guns. Everybody held their breath and kept watch as the robots moved along the perimeter. They were just about out of sight, and Captain Stack began to get up. Again, Johansen shook his head and told him to wait.

The robots froze. Then came the flashing red lights and alarm. Giggs was shaking, hugging tightly to his briefcase. On the far side of the Rocket Garden there came a rustling from the trees. The robots spun on it and opened fire, splintering trees and ripping down the branches. After a moment, they stopped firing and the smoke settled. They waited long seconds before moving on. Once they were behind the next building, an alligator lumbered out into the open as if nothing had happened.

"Man, those things are tough!" chuckled Evans.

Johansen told him, "But not too smart. The robot patrols come by every four hours, on the dot. And every time, one of the gators thinks its food and tries to get it. You can set your watch by it. Must be a nest or something over there. They're not all as lucky as that one."

"Focus!" Stack warned. "So, four-hour rotations and a gator nest. Got it. Anything else?"

"No, Sir. I couldn't get inside the buildings without going into the open, so I don't know what's waiting in there. But other than the patrols, it's dead quiet out here."

"Copy that, Sergeant. Okay, Doc, you're up. We'll cover you, but watch your six, just the same. Be back here in exactly three-hours and fifty minutes."

One of the mechanics spoke up, "There's no way we can do this in less than four hours."

"Three hours and fifty minutes exactly! Not a second more. Unless you have a better idea, we'll just have to let the next patrol pass and then repeat the process. If you don't finish by sun up, we come back tomorrow night. And if need be, the night after that. We do whatever it takes, as many times as it takes to get that thing off the ground. Got it?"

It had actually gotten very quiet throughout the compound in the hours since the New Mexico team left. The delegates were all gathered in the War-Room, making final preparations for the space crew before they rolled out.

Jackson wandered into the mess hall, hoping to have a safe, quiet meal with Daniel for the first time in a very long time. Aside from the stray scientists guzzling coffee and odd soldiers scattered here and there, the hall was largely empty.

The training level seemed like the obvious alternative, but again, mostly deserted. A group of soldiers were playing basketball with the small squad of apes staying behind.

On to the next. The loading dock was exactly the opposite. Troops loading trucks and astronauts – both human and simian – prepping and packing their equipment. But once again, no Daniel. Which probably made sense, given that he had also opted not to see the other team off.

The next spot was the behavioral testing level where Jackson found Grant playing 3-D chess and getting his butt handed to him by Darwin. They hadn't seen Daniel either.

Tired and frustrated, Jackson went back to the apes' barracks level. And guess what; no Daniel. Only his journal sitting on his empty bunk. Jackson sighed as the realization came. "Oh, kiddo. Please tell me you didn't." He sat down and started reading.

Inside a machine shop, the mechanics were connecting enormous hoses, end to end. Giggs was working at a map with the Captain. "This is going too slowly. My team needs at least twelve more hours to finish the hose. Then we'll need to run it from the tanks - two buildings out that way – to the rocket, three hundred yards in the complete opposite direction."

"And how long to transfer the fuel?", Stack asked.

"Anywhere between five and eight hours if we could use the mechanical pumps."

Captain Stack checked his watch. "Well, we can't use the machinery, so how long?"

Giggs thought for a minute and shrugged. "We're going to have to pump it manually, while simultaneously making the repairs on the rocket and installing the winch… Which hopefully won't generate any sparks and blow up the whole thing. So, best guess, eighteen hours."

"Okay, I need to telegraph back to command with an update. It'll take at least a few days for the flight crew to ship out and get here. Use that time to figure it out. We have nineteen minutes to get back to cover, and after the patrol passes, your team can get back at it. When the time comes, my men can start pumping in fifteen-minute shifts. For now, we move out in eleven minutes".

...and I can't even pretend that dad would have ever been okay with me going into space. But still... It's just not fair!

There were a million things going through Jackson's mind as he read his son's journal. Not the least of which was guilt for doing just that. And then he read the final passage.

I know what you're thinking, dad. Don't do that. I left this so that you'd find it. I knew you'd only read it because you're worried. It's okay. Really. I'm not mad. Which is exactly what I'm asking you. Please, don't be mad at me. I know you don't understand. I know you just want to keep me safe, but I had to go.

I couldn't tell you before, because I knew you'd try to stop me. But I couldn't leave without saying anything. If I don't make it back, I want you to know how proud I am that you're my father. Sure, we never went to the movies, I have no idea how to play baseball or football. But you taught me to survive. You taught me how to protect myself and the people I love. The first person on that list is you, dad. I love you and couldn't stand to lose you like we did mom. That's why I have to do this. Because I'll do whatever I possibly can to protect you.

The only thing that Jackson didn't feel at all, was surprise. But among all the other things he was in fact feeling - fear, guilt, desperation - two more emotions joined the list: Fatherly pride and new-found determination.

The caravan had gotten off the road into the woods. Several apes had perched themselves high up in the branches to stand watch, while their human counterparts covered the low ground. Dr. Goodwin was going over maps and alternate routes with Captain Lindt. The rest of the team were eating while they had the chance.

Hercules took some fruit and headed back to his transport truck. He climbed up into the back and stuffed the food under a pile of body-armor before taking a seat beside it. The pile shifted and Hercules patted it gently.

"How did you know?" Daniel asked as he sat up to eat. Hercules snorted a laugh and signed. "It was the smell…. And I'm not stupid."

"Yeah, I'm not stupid either," Goodwin said from the back of the truck.

Daniel pushed off the rest of the gear and sat up on the bench beside Hercules. "Please, don't send me back or anything. I need to be part of this. I need to…"

"Save it, kid." She cut him off. "There's no way I'd send you back on your own, and it's too late to turn around. But first chance we get, I'll have to get a message to your Dad. He's going to freak out. That is, if he's not already freaking out because… Well, HIS SON IS GONE!! What were you thinking?"

Daniel's eyes were locked firmly on the floor in shame. "He knows. I told him where I was going."

She was aghast. "Wait, what? I have a hard time believing he'd be okay with this. Look, I like you, kid but I can't tell you how pissed I am that you'd lie to me."

"I didn't lie to you. I did tell him… Sorta'." The doctor's eyes narrowed and Daniel swore he could feel them burning into him. "I left him a note. It'll be fine."

She groaned and did her best to chew back a tirade. After composing herself, "Here's the deal. You do not leave Herc's side. When the fighting starts, and it most certainly will, you do whatever you need to stay out of it. I'm pretty sure you're not an idiot, maybe just a bit selfish. In case you forgot, we're trying to save the world here, and I can't have this team distracted by worrying about keeping you safe."

"You know I can take care of myself!" he snapped.

"All I really know is that you'd be dead twice-over if it wasn't for us! So, stay down, stay covered and stay out of this! End of discussion!" Daniel was crushed as she stormed off. And if he could see her face, he'd have known that she was too.

Hercules nudged him and signed, "You'll be safe with me. For the record, I think you made the right decision. If you tried going to space? Now, that would have been dumb." And offered the kid a fist bump.

Two of the mechanics checked to make sure the coast was clear. Once certain, they began dragging an end of the fueling hose from the machine shop. It was heavy and slow going. Slower still because they were terrified of being found by the robots. Johansen, the sniper and two other soldiers covered them from the tree line and a rooftop.

Inside the building, Giggs and the others rooted around for anything useful to make repairs on the rocket. "One-hour, twenty-seven minutes", Captain Stack called out.

"Shhh! Are you crazy?" Giggs scolded him. "They're going to hear you!"

"That's just the thing, Doc. Why haven't they so far? I've been thinking about it. Four-hour patrol rotations seems pretty light. All the security cameras everywhere and they haven't seen us? This whole time we've been here, and no engagement at all? Security on the whole just feels lax. I can't help but wonder if this is some sort of trap."

"Or maybe they've just underestimated us." Giggs countered.

"Again, doesn't that strike you as odd? Have you seen pretty much the whole planet? It didn't get this way by them underestimating us. They've been ahead of us the whole time."

"So, you're saying we should abort?"

"We can't abort. No, we carry on with the mission but keep alert. Assume that we're being set up, act accordingly and be ready. Now, where are we with the rocket?"

Giggs checked his notes, "As soon as they get the fuel hose attached at both ends, we can start pumping. Fortunately, the ship wasn't bolted or welded to the stand. There are simple clamps holding it in place. We just need to open them before launch. Preliminary checks show that the seals appear to be in good condition as is most of the wiring. There isn't any damage to the circuit boards other than needing a good cleaning, so we're good there. But the main stage combustion ignitor was corroded and won't fire."

"What does that mean? Can you fix it or not?" the Captain asked.

"A combustion ignitor uses an electric charge to spark the fuel. We can't fix the one that's in there, but one of the other rockets likely has one we can use to replace it."

"Wait, so, we just have to change the spark plugs?"

"It's called the Main Stage Combustion ignitor, but essentially, yes. Most of these rockets were built by the same government contractors, so they should use a lot of the same parts."

"Fine. Whatever. Just stay alert and get it done." He checked his watch again, "One-hour, twenty-minutes."

As Stack went to brief his men, Giggs went back to the tool bench and opened his briefcase and the computer within. He opened the options menu and clicked, "Connect to wi-fi".

ON THE ROAD

Days had passed since Jackson stole a horse and set out after his son. He travelled light and was able to make pretty good speed on his own. It turned out that he was a pretty good tracker, too. Probably in part due to the fact that this wasn't his first time having to go after Daniel.

A couple of wrong turns aside, Jackson picked up their trail somewhere around Charleston and followed it almost all the way to Little Rock. At that point, he actually resorted to flipping a coin as to whether the caravan stayed to the north, through Oklahoma, or further south towards Dallas. North it was. They probably wouldn't want to go near any larger cities anyway. He was exhausted and decided to stop for rest near Wichita Falls.

At the very least, he knew where they were headed and could catch up with them there. Hopefully before they engaged the enemy.

OFF THE COAST OF FLORIDA

The flight team's boat cautiously came upon the one belonging to the repair crew. They found it empty, calmly bobbing on the tide. Dr. Jepson scanned the coastline through binoculars. "There, in the brush. Rafts."

Lieutenant John Hicks took the glasses from him to inspect the landing site. Of course, in the darkness it was hard to see anything at all, but the fact that he couldn't see any people was unsettling.

"Should we anchor here, like they did?" Jepson asked.

Hicks thought a moment before answering. "No. We still have no idea what happened here, but something tells me we may need to make a quick getaway. We take this in to the beach and turn it so it's ready. Leave their boat where it is as a back-up. For all we know, they're fine and simply keeping out of sight."

"I'm just saying, the repair team never checked in when they were supposed to." Jepson countered.

"They didn't check in before we left. That doesn't mean they never called at all. So, we do this carefully. Give Stack and his crew the benefit of the doubt. Last thing we need, is to rush headlong into friendly fire."

Fifteen minutes later, they came upon the prior team's now decimated camp. The equipment had been smashed, including the telegraph. Ammunition casings were scattered everywhere among tire treads and what could only be described as robotic footprints.

"Okay, now I'm a little worried." Hicks muttered.

"Listen, we don't know what's out there or what shape the rocket is in but we can't just stay here and ponder," Jepson tried his best to sound confident. "Let me send the apes on ahead to check it out before we go in."

"Negative. We all go together. Those apes are assets of the highest priority, and we can't afford to lose them or the other astronauts. My men aren't rocket scientists, so, we need the flight crew to put eyes on the craft. You and your team just stay close and stay low. Let us deal with any enemy opposition."

Reaching the main compound, the flight crew could plainly see the fuel hose attached to the rocket and equipment scattered across the grounds. However, there was no sign of the repair team anywhere. No robots either, for that matter. Several small craters and scorch marks on the walls made it clear that there had been a firefight.

A small stone pinged off the side of Lt. Hicks' head. He spun, weapon drawn. It was Johansen who had thrown it from his rooftop perch. He held up a single finger to quiet the newcomers before sliding down a drainpipe to meet them. "You need to find cover and get out of here, fast! Patrols are coming every fifteen minutes since the attack. Four robots per rotation. I think they got everybody else. Unless…. Did you see anyone on your way in? It was crazy, I lost track of all of them!"

"Calm down, sergeant. Tell me exactly what happened here. What about the rocket? Is it ready? Can we still launch?"

SOUTHWEST SATELLITE ARRAY

Jackson stood at the fence overlooking the vast field of satellite dishes. The grass around him was tall enough to keep him pretty much hidden. And that's precisely what he was hoping the infiltration team was doing. The alternative was that they simply weren't there, which in turn brought up the question, why? Did something go wrong on the way? Did the robots get them? Panic was beginning to get the better of him.

Within the satellite field, robots were everywhere. Running sweeps up and down the rows of dishes.

"Get down before they see you!" Came the woman's voice from the trees behind him. Jackson nearly jumped out of his skin at the sound. He slowly turned and saw Dr. Goodwin waving him over from her hiding spot. As his brain cleared a bit, he ran in a crouch to her.

Jackson began rambling a mile a minute, "Oh my God, you're alright! What happened? How did I beat you here? Are you really alright? Where's Daniel, Is he okay? How could you let him come? I need to see him! What's going on here?"

She clamped a hand over his mouth while pulling him behind the trees. "Stop. Just breathe. We're all fine, Daniel is fine. I'll explain everything, but not here. For now, you have to just shut up, keep low and follow me back to camp."

The old ranch had been razed mostly to the ground. The main house tilted and leaned on what little remained of its outer wall. As they approached, Jackson heard the audible clicks of several weapons.

"Friendlies. Stand down," Goodwin called out and signed simultaneously.

"You need to eat something and catch your breath," she told Jackson. But he wasn't listening. Instead, he ran, practically bowling over apes and soldiers alike, to get to his son.

Daniel was a mix of both ashamed and relieved as he gave his dad a big hug. "What are you doing here? You should have stayed in the bunker where it's safe."

Jackson squeezed the boy tighter than he ever had before, tears in his eyes. "Idiot kid, how could you know I'd read your journal, but not think I'd come after you?"

"I'm sorry, Dad. I knew you'd try to stop me if I told you beforehand. I just had to do this. Before you say anything, don't blame Dr. Goodwin or the others. I snuck on the truck. They didn't know. She was pretty mad at me, but I'm not going back."

"I figured," Jackson answered. "But I can't stand the thought of losing you. So, we do this together. No more tricks, no more lies. Deal?"

The rest of the troops were holed up in the remnants of the barn. Jackson and Daniel found Dr. Goodwin going over schematics of the satellite array with Captain Lindt. "So, what's the plan? How do we help?"

The Doctor eyed them both in frustration. "I'm guessing that taking your son and going back is out of the question?"

"Have you met my son?", Jackson countered.

The Captain interrupted, "My men and the Doctor's team are trained for this. The best thing you two can do is just stay out of the way."

"Yeah," Goodwin continued. "Clearly Lindt doesn't know Daniel too well. So, here's the deal. The telegraph is wired into an old phone line, over there. The plan was to wait until we got confirmation of the launch, and then go in and take out the dishes before the A.I. can send a signal to attack it. But we haven't heard anything from anybody. Last night, the robots went on high alert, so we have to assume that they know something is up. A quiet in-and-out operation is no longer an option, so, we're going to give it until tonight and hit them hard. The apes will engage and distract the robots. Captain Lindt has a suitcase Electro-Magnetic Pulse weapon with about a half-mile radius. Theoretically, that'll shut down all the dishes and robots at once. It won't be pretty and might not work. Not to sound like General Ford, I can't give you odds on survival, but at least I can make sure you understand what you're getting yourselves into and leave the choice to you."

"I thought the general said we couldn't use an EMP," Jackson said.

"No, the robots couldn't," Lindt chimed in. "The delegates had decided that we shouldn't use them in areas where we relied on machines or technology for daily life. This place is far enough away from anything that it was worth the sacrifice. The hope was that when this is over, we can get the world back up and running as it was before."

"Thereby having not learned from our history, be doomed to repeat it?" Jackson asked sarcastically. "So, why not just throw it over the fence and set it off from a distance?"

"Negative. The main circuits and connections are in a bunker in the center. Schematics show it goes five-levels underground. There's a lot of space and concrete between us and them. Again, this is a relatively weak EMP. We have to get inside to make sure we destroy everything."

"I'm telling you, Sir, it was nuts. We were here for days with no contact. We learned their patterns, did everything right. And then WHAM! Out of nowhere, their patterns changed. It's like they suddenly knew what we were up to and were waiting for us!"

Johansen was nearly hysterical. The flight team had taken him and made camp in a completely different location than the first. And that's when he told them his story.

*****

Roughly eighteen hours earlier, the crew went about their missions. The mechanics had been working on the rocket while the soldiers did their shifts pumping fuel. Every four-hours, taking cover as the patrols passed.

They were just returning to position, Johansen manning the pump when the first shots rang out. Staying low, he ran back to the edge of the building. From there, he could see one of the mechanics backing away from a robot, out near the rocket. Two soldiers were firing at the robot, trying to cover his escape. Just then, a second robot swooped in, grabbing one of the soldiers in a mechanical claw. The man was lifted off the ground and flung off, out of Johansen's view.

Three more robots were spreading out to cover more ground. The cat was clearly out of the bag and noise, no longer an issue. Lieutenant Evans bolted from behind the hedge encircling the Rocket Garden and tossed a grenade. The explosion knocked the robot on its side, but not for long.

One of the robots snatched up a mechanic and stuffed him inside some sort of canister within its own frame.

Captain Stack shepherded Dr. Giggs, still clutching the briefcase, into the replica of a command module and slammed the hatch closed behind him. He then took up a firing position to fight off the enemy.

Johansen slung his sniper rifle over his shoulder, in favor of the rocket launcher left lying on the pavement by one of the others. It was loaded, but he would only get one shot. Even as he ran, he was scanning for the best target. He didn't want to blow up the robot that he knew held a mechanic prisoner. In truth, he had lost track of most of his teammates, and couldn't know if or which of the robots had people in their bellies.

The Captain now ran across the open ground, being chased and weaving to avoid gunfire from a robot. Johansen watched through the launcher's reticle as Stack passed under the decommissioned Space Shuttle, Champion. The robot was too large to go under, and stopped just short of crashing into it.

Johansen hoped that the Captain kept running out the other side because this was his best and only option. "Fire in the hole!" He shouted as he squeezed the trigger.

The explosion was massive. All the other craft rattled and lurched at the concussion. Space Shuttle and robot parts rained down everywhere. A thick cloud of smoke covered everything. It was impossible to see inches in any direction.

*****

"And that was it. Maybe the robots thought we were all finished in the explosion, but it got really quiet. I managed to get back up on the rooftop for a vantage, but I couldn't find anybody... Until you showed up, that is. Your rocket seems undamaged. Well, as undamaged as it was before the attack, at least."

"How close to launch ready is it?" asked Jepson.

"Unknown, sir," Johansen answered. "We were fueling it, but the mechanics were still tinkering until they were.... You know."

"Okay, at ease soldier. We'll take it from here," Hicks said. "Doctor, when it's safe, you and the astronauts will do as best an inspection as you can. The rest of us will provide cover and search for survivors. We need to do this quick. Hopefully the robots will either think we've given up and gone, or that they got us all."

"They definitely didn't get us all," said Captain Stack as he came into the camp. He was dragging Dr. Giggs by the scruff of his neck, and shoved him to the ground in the middle. "But we've got a bigger problem. Lieutenant, did your team happen to bring another telegraph? Ours seems to have been destroyed."

An aide came barging into the War-Room, waving a piece of paper. "We've got big problems!" Everybody turned to see what the commotion was, but it was so crowded that the aide couldn't get through. "Please, you have to hear this! We're in danger!"

The general tried to get to the aide from his end, and whatever she was trying to show them. Finally, Darwin took the matter into his own hands. He jumped up and swung from the overhead lights across the room. He grabbed the paper from the aide and handed it back to the general.

After reading it, General Ford handed it off to the president of the United States, whose jaw nearly hit the floor. He passed it on to the Chinese president beside him, who had much the same reaction. On and on, delegate after delegate. Murmurs and grumbles from the crowd. Frustrated, Ford went to the podium and yelled, "Everybody be quiet! Listen up! We've just gotten word that the team in Florida has met with heavy opposition." Everyone gasped at the news. "We know that some of them have evaded the enemy, but the status of the rocket and the mission is unknown. However, the news gets worse from there. We have it on good authority that the robots now know where we are, and are heading towards us."

The delegates erupted into chaos again, each trying to shout over the next. "We have to evacuate! Where do we go?" shrieked the French leader.

"Well," said the general, keeping his face impassive. "This is it. This compound was our fallback position. There is no place, and as far as we know, no time to retreat. That's the bad news. The good news is that this is the most secure facility on the planet. Even if they do know where we are, once they get here, they'll have to get through our defenses and then dig through a mile-an-a-half of earth, concrete and steel to get in."

"You can't expect us to just sit tight and wait!" argued the Russian Prime Minister.

"Not at all," Ford answered. "We fight. We gather every person we have to defend our position for as long as we can... And we hope that our field teams can somehow complete their objectives."

"It seems we have a traitor in our company," the Captain said as he handed the briefcase to Jepson. Giggs averted his eyes as the whole team surrounded him. Upon opening the case and seeing the laptop, Jepson's eyes went wide. After a quick inspection, he gasped and threw it into the brush.

"We need to get out of here! He was connected to wi-fi. They can track us!" he shouted. "Giggs, why would you do this?"

"Because we can't win this war. Tell me something, do you know what they're doing with the humans? Have you noticed that there are no bodies left behind? I'd rather be a pet than cattle."

"What is he talking about," asked Li Wei Liu, the medic. "What are they doing with the humans? Does that mean they're still alive?"

Giggs stayed silent as they all waited for an answer. Finally, Andreyev smacked him across the back of the head. "Answer the question, Doctor. Before going to space, I was with the KGB. I'm out of practice, but I'll make you talk."

"Don't you see? It's too late. The planet belongs to them. I was told to bring you to them and they would take care of me."

"I say we give him to them!" Johansen interjected. "Strap a bomb to him and send him right to their leader!" He grabbed the doctor by the collar, jerking him to his feet. "How can we even trust the work that his mechanics were doing? We need to..."

"That's enough, soldier!" Lieutenant Hicks shouted. "First things first. We need answers. Giggs, did you or your men sabotage the rocket in any way?"

"No! The others didn't even know I was talking to the robots. They were the ones doing the work on the rocket. I never laid a hand on it."

"I don't believe him," Andreyev said while cracking his knuckles. "Not yet, anyway. But when I'm through, I'm sure he'll tell the truth."

Giggs squirmed and tried to back away from the large Russian. Instead, he only managed to bump into Bella and Conan. Have you ever seen a really angry baboon? Much more frightening than an astronaut. A human astronaut, that is. And still, far less intimidating than Bella. "Ooh, scree, ahh ooh, ahh ook!" she said through gnashed teeth. The other apes laughed. The humans didn't know what she said, since she didn't sign it. But it was along the lines of the humans taking too long in making him soil himself.

"Stand down. All of you." Hicks continued. "He'll tell the truth, because he's going up there with you."

"What? No. That wasn't the plan. I can't go into space." The doctor was panicking.

"That's just it, Giggs. You ruined the old plan when you sold us out to your masters. So, I'm improvising. Since we've seen how far you're willing to go to stay alive, that's the only way we can trust you. Whatever happens to the flight crew, happens to you too. Got it? The rest of you, pack up. We're moving out. Leave his briefcase here. Maybe the robots will track it and that will get some of them away from the Rocket Garden. Make no mistake here. We are on borrowed time. We go in hard and we go in A.S.A.P. The robots won't expect it. That's the lesson we need to take from our ape counterparts. That's what will give us a chance."

Captain Stack and Johansen shared a look, both impressed by the Lieutenant.

The telegraph operator once again handed messages to General Ford. This time, however, his reaction was far less grim. "Listen up, everybody! We've just gotten word that both teams are alive and in position. Looks like it's game on. At this point it's simply a race to the finish. Best we can do here is stick to our guns and stay alive. Our fate is entirely in their hands now."

Darwin tugged on Grant's sleeve. He began signing frantically. "Whoa, slow down there, buddy. I'm not as good at this as you yet." Grant said.

Darwin sighed in frustration. He began again, slower this time as if speaking to an infant. Grant nodded his understanding as the ape laid out his idea. "That's insane!" Grant signed back. "I am so totally onboard!" And then high-fived Darwin.

The pair fought their way through the crowded room. "Dad! I mean, General... Sir!" and finally they reached him up front. "I think we can help them!"

General Ford was skeptical. "I don't see how. We're hundreds of miles from either team, buried in a concrete box deep underground, and with God knows how many robots heading here to get us. We need everybody focused on keeping that from happening."

"No, I get all that, Dad. And that's just it, you don't need to do anything. Darwin and I can do this by ourselves... Well, we'll need the telegraph guy to show us the way, but that's all."

When Grant finished explaining, Ford replied, "That's insane. There's no reason to expect that to work."

"I know, right?" Grant answered. "My words exactly. But that's also exactly what makes it so brilliant!"

"Brilliant may be a bit optimistic. This is really the best you could come up with?"

"No, Darwin came up with it. And actually, so did you! Dad, this is why you called Mom and the apes in the first place. To defy expectations. They're unpredictable."

"I don't know, Grant. It seems risky."

Grant's eyes went wide in surprise. "You mean like stealing an antique rocket with a team of apes to storm a space station? What are you afraid of, that the robots will find our hideout? Don't you see? This is the very definition of button-mashing!"

Just then a soldier barged in, "Sir, our spotters just reported the first wave of robots approaching the perimeter!"

The general sighed. "Well then, what have we got to lose?"

Grant wasted no time. He headed out with Darwin and the Telegraph operator, calling out over his shoulder, "Get your troops ready, and wait for the signal! You'll know it when you see it!"

Robots were no longer patrolling. They now stood sentry around the grounds. Additionally, the team spotted a pair of drones circling the airspace above.

"Well, this makes things more complicated," Stack muttered to himself before continuing. "Giggs, what's the status of the rocket? How much time do we need to be launch ready?"

Giggs was still nearly paralyzed in fear. He shook his head as he thought it over. "I, I don't know," he stuttered. "The hoses look like they're still attached and they were nearly done fueling it, but we still needed to find and replace a part."

"Wait!" Stack said, reaching into his pack. "The spark plug thingy, right?" And he held up a part, roughly the size of a football. "One of your mechanics was able to snag it during the fight and hand it off before he was taken."

"Main Stage Combustion ignitor," Giggs corrected.

"It's a spark plug," Astronaut Mike Rodgers said. "Johnston and I can replace it."

With a shrug, Giggs answered "Then I would say it could be flight ready in about four hours, without interference from the robots. But seeing as that's not going to happen, this whole thing is a suicide mission."

"Johansen, can you take out the drones?" Stack asked.

"Sir, I can definitely get one, at least. But I'd have to be fast to get both before they know what's going on. I'm talking near impossible kind of fast. And they're not even moving in straight lines."

"Take Private Murray with you. He's a good shot. One drone apiece, synchronized shots." Hicks ordered. "We still have to figure out how to deal with the robots on the ground."

"Leave that to us," Jepson said, surrounded by his apes who were eager for a fight."

"Good. Astronauts, start flight prep. The rest of you, take shifts at the fuel pump. If you're not fueling, you're fighting, copy? Giggs, you're up first," the lieutenant commanded. "I want this bird in the air in two-hours."

"I told you, four hours!" Giggs argued.

"You sure did," was Hicks' response. "But I don't trust you, so you get two. Everybody, move out."

The best they could hope for was that the satellite team was faring better than they were.

They most certainly were not faring any better than the others.

Private Tapper crawled on his belly beneath one of the dishes. Most of the robots were too big to be effective in the small spaces, so they were concentrated on the outer perimeters. Drones were also useless other than for recon. Apes were swarming the fences and hopping from dish-to-dish while the humans tried to make their way to the concrete control bunker. At every turn, they seemed to find themselves cut off.

Daniel ran and slid under one of the robots, tossing a grenade above him as he went. The explosion blew off the robot's leg causing it to topple.

Hercules was hanging onto the top of one robot, when a second swiped what looked like an arm made from the telescoping neck of a crane. The great ape was flung into a dish, knocking it out of alignment.

A chimpanzee had managed to pry open a robot's circuit panel and was randomly yanking wires as it spun and bucked like a rodeo bull.

Gunfire and shrapnel tore through the air in all directions. At best it was a stalemate between the tides of robots and apes.

ROLLING THUNDER DRIVE-IN THEATRE

General Ford himself peeked over the concession counter into the vast parking lot. From there, he could see four combat robots encircling drilling and excavation machines. For some reason, they were stopped off to the side of the lot.

The general ducked back down out of sight and whispered to the Secret Service agent beside him, "I can't figure out why there aren't more of them or what they're waiting for, but we're going to need explosives for that drill, and there's an armed escort that we'll need to handle first."

And then they heard it. The large growl of engines. Plane engines. Two B-2 bombers passed over head.

"Strike that. Get below, take cover, fast! This is going to be bad!"

A.G.D.A. BUNKER SERVICE LEVEL

Far below, the telegraph operator led Grant and Darwin as they wound their way through the narrow corridors on the lowest levels of the compound. The walls were lined with ducts for all the wires and cables of the whole place. They followed the ducts, leading to the end point in the breaker room.

The door was a solid slab of metal with a key code pad and retinal scanner. None of them would have the authorization to enter… even if they were connected to the servers behind the door. The telegraph operator noticed the other two staring at him expectantly. "What? I'm just a communications officer. Don't look at me."

Grant thought for a minute. "If we could get into the panel, I might be able to hack it."

"Clearly, they didn't have a robot invasion in mind when they designed the system," Telegraph Guy said. "Wait, the wall ducts carry all the inbound lines, but the outputs all run under the floor. It's hollow. If we find an access point, maybe we can go under."

"With all this security, I somehow doubt it would be that easy." Grant scoffed.

"For you and me, maybe," the operator said. "But I can't imagine apes were any more of a security consideration than robots."

"I'm not much of a computer guy," Darwin signed.

"Good point. But I don't have any better ideas, pal. If you can get in, there's got to be a way to open it from the inside."

The trio backtracked about a quarter-mile along the corridor before they found the bolted hatch in the floor. Grant used a multi-tool to undo the bolts and lifted the hatch. It was dark below and crowded with wires.

"Okay, Darwin, it'll be tight, but if you just follow the cables, it should lead straight in."

Darwin climbed down into the floor. He would have to lie on his back and shimmy along the lines the whole way.

"What could possibly go wrong?" He signed.

"You'll be fine," Grant returned. "This is going to work. Trust me, it'll be fine."

And once the chimp was out of view, Grant asked the telegraph operator, "It'll be fine, right? This is going to work?"

While the operator shrugged that he didn't know, the wail of alarms answered rather definitively!

The drones flew in opposing figure eight patterns, crossing directly over the Saturn V. On the ground, Stack held Giggs beside a wall, ready to run for the fuel pump. Giggs' hands were zip-tied in front of him. "Don't even think of calling out to your friends, Doc."

"They're not my friends! They were a chance to survive this war, a means to an end."

"Wrong! I'm your ONLY chance to survive. And you better believe I have the means to end you if you try anything. When I say go, you get to that pump and put your back into it. So help me, if I even think you're not doing…"

"Yes. I get it, Captain."

Jepson anxiously awaited alongside Andreyev and Li to make a break for the rocket's hatch, while Johnston and Rodgers got ready to run to the main stage thruster compartment.

Johansen and Murray were in position on the rooftop, each following their assigned target through their scopes. Lieutenant Hicks was behind them on overwatch. "Steady. Last thing we need is them crashing into the rocket."

"Copy that, sir," Murray said.

Johansen rolled his eyes. "Not my first rodeo, sir."

"What was that, Sergeant?"

"Um, I said, copy that, sir."

"Right," Hicks intoned as he watched the ground through binoculars. "Stand by for distraction, and…"

That's when the apes stormed out of the bushes, screaming and making as much noise as they could. Both drones locked on and changed course-heading straight at them.

"Clear!" shouted Johansen. Firing in two… One… Now!" He and Murray squeezed the triggers in unison. His round found the sweet spot in the craft's battery, and it exploded in air.

Murray's shot, while still effective, only managed to hit one of the target's rotors. The drone spun off to the side before crashing into a nearby standing rocket. One of the cables holding it in place snapped and the rocket listed to its side, leaning against the Saturn V.

"Um, my bad?" Murry said. The two snipers immediately turned to providing cover fire.

There was no going back now. Each of the smaller teams sprang into action. Stack shoved Giggs - who nearly fell over - towards the fuel pump.

The apes turned their attention to the standing robots who were now attacking. This gave the astronauts their opportunity to get to the Saturn rocket.

The first bombs hit with the magnitude of an earthquake. Luckily the installation had been built to withstand a nuclear attack, but even that far below ground level, it could be felt. Everything shook and lights flickered.

The delegates all huddled together, under tables. "Where is General Ford? Is there any word from the defense team that went up there?" the president of the United States shouted. "Is there any way to see what's going on up there?"

*****

Down in the bowels of the compound, Grant was trying to see into the darkness of the sub flooring. "Darwin? Are you okay in there?"

"Ooh, Scree! Ahh, ook!" came back, muffled by the distance.

"What'd he say?" the telegraph operator asked.

"No Idea. I don't speak ape," Grant answered, relieved. "But at least he said something."

Another explosion from above shook the bunker. The ceiling cracked and a large section gave way. Grant shoved the telegraph operator out of its path, "You need to get back up there and keep the communications gear in working order! Go! We've got this!"

The frightened operator ran back to the stairs. That's when Grant turned back and saw that the huge slab of concrete had smashed the floor where they stood seconds ago. The access point was crushed and buried.

"No!" In a panic, he began trying futilely to clear the rubble. "Darwin! If you can hear me, I'm coming, Buddy! Please, say something, give me a sign! Darwin? Please answer!"

A couple dozen scattered dishes had been taken down, but that was nothing among the hundreds that still stood.

Hercules bounded across the ground, knocking out the legs of the taller robots. A swarm of chimps worked at it from the top. They jumped from dish to dish while firing at and ripping the circuits out of the enemy.

Captain Lindt led Dr. Goodwin and two soldiers through the maze of satellite relays, but the control bunker seemed barely closer than it had been earlier.

Jackson watched his son. It was almost impossible for him to remember the little boy he'd once been. And as much as he tried, there was no way he could keep up. He was out of breath and propped himself against one of the dish posts, firing at an encroaching robot. In the distance, he could see the other humans pinned down. He had to do something to help.

The apes were working their way inwards from the perimeter. The robots were closing ranks, defending the bunker while the humans were pinned down in the center of a slowly shrinking ring of enemies.

Daniel was fast, staying low and firing at the joints in the robots' armor. Fighting side by side with the apes, he even seemed to move like them. Easily slipping around and between the enemies. He made his way towards Dr. Goodwin and the others.

Even if the apes were to ultimately defeat the robots, Jackson saw no way for those trapped in the center to escape, unharmed. And now, seeing his son rushing to join them in certain death, he sprang into action.

True to his word, Hercules did all he could to protect Daniel by fighting beside him, clearing his path where he could. As a robot exploded above them, Hercules shielded the boy from shrapnel with his own body.

Jackson shrieked when he saw his son and the gorilla hit the ground. Everything else seemed to fade from his view as he ran to them. Hercules was lying on his belly, alive and shaking his head clear. He growled in surprise when Jackson grabbed him by the arm and tried in vain to lift him.

From underneath the massive furry body came a groan. Hercules lifted his weight up and Daniel spat out dirt and fur. "Thanks, big guy," he said.

Hercules signed back, "Told you I'd keep you safe." The boy laughed and asked, "Now can you get off me? You weigh a ton."

"That's going to be a problem," Rodgers said, looking at the new obstacle.

"One thing at a time," Johnston replied. "Let's get this part installed and then we'll deal with that."

Andreyev and Jepson felt the impact from inside the capsule. "What was that?" Jepson asked.

"No idea," Andreyev answered. "Li, go check it out. Jepson, you focus on our job."

Kong, the tiny monkey, had snuck back and grabbed Giggs' briefcase. It was still powered up and connected to the wi-fi. Dragging it with his tail, he ran willy-nilly around the compound, getting robots to chase him away from the rocket.

Bella leapt from the top of another standing rocket, onto the domed head of an enemy and opened fire.

Giggs' arms were throbbing from pumping fuel. "Please, I can't keep going like this."

Stack - positioned in the doorway taking pot shots at the robots - was less than sympathetic. "That's too bad, traitor. Keep pumping. I'd hate for you not to have enough fuel to get where you're going."

"It would go faster if you had one of your soldiers take over."

"Fine," the Captain grinned. "Your other choice is to grab a weapon, go out there and fight. Otherwise, just shut up and pump the gas!"

Astro and Snot were on the ground, hopping up and down, pointing and signing frantically until they caught Conan's attention. Whatever they were saying, he nodded his understanding.

The baboon launched himself from atop an abandoned churro stand to the Saturn V. He grabbed the frayed cable and swung it like a lasso. He spotted Titus ping-ponging about as a confused robot fired at him wildly. "Scree! Ook ma ooh Ahh!" Conan shouted to the chimpanzee as he threw the cable.

Titus caught the cable in mid-air as he dove between the robot's legs. He hit the ground in a roll and righted himself. The robot turned around and around, trying to take aim at the ape beneath it, but Titus stayed in as close as he could, wrapping the cable around the mechanical ankle.

Once it was secure, the chimp climbed up the leg and body to the robot's head. He punched at it and jumped. Robots don't show emotions, but it would be a pretty safe bet that this one was really pissed. The machine opened fire as Titus ran off, but the zig-zagging ape managed to avoid being hit. So, the robot gave chase.

The cable pulled taught, nearly tripping the robot. It steadied itself and tried to pull free of the snare. There came a groan of metal as its leg took a step. The second step was a bit less of a strain, but there was another groan.

The fallen rocket began to roll off the side of the Saturn V. It hit the ground and continued rolling, coiling the cable as it went. The robot tried to pull free, but it was too late. The rocket crashed into the metal soldier, sweeping out its legs and tearing off its foot as it fell to the ground.

Lt. Hicks ran towards the edge of the rooftop, calling behind him as he climbed down, "The rocket is clear! I'm going to open those clamps for launch! Cover me!"

Kong was quite literally the monkey in the middle. Flanked by two robots who had him dead to rights. Instead, he hurled the briefcase straight up above him. The robots opened fire as it passed between them, managing to blow each other to pieces.

Jepson and Andreyev jumped out of the command module and found Li hiding next to the stand. "It doesn't look like there's any damage to the rocket. It was incredible! You should've…".

"Okay, okay. You can tell us once we're in flight." Andreyev interrupted. "Where are the others? Did they get the ignitor replaced?"

Rodgers poked his head out from a hatch just above them. "Just finished. Soon as we're finished fueling, we can light this candle."

The twins were being chased along the outer perimeter. It had started as trying to lure the robots away, but fast became a case of running for their lives. The robots stopped in their tracks when Snot grabbed Astro and pulled him into the swampy brush.

There was a flurry of splashing and growling and the screams of monkeys from the bushes. The robots fired wildly into the thicket until the noise died down and then turned to walk away.

Bella froze in horror. She and the twins had been like family since birth. With a mighty roar, she attacked! Titus, Kong and Conan had never heard her scream like that. They jumped into the fray beside her. In a frenzy, the four apes fought like a hundred!

This was their chance. Andreyev climbed back into the command module and ordered the others to fall back to the machine shop and assist in the fueling. The soldiers joined in with the apes, hammering the enemy.

"How much longer?" Jepson shouted out as they entered the building.

Stack shoved Giggs and replied, "Should be about ten more minutes, if he'll quit whining and just get it done."

Johnston ran over and knocked Giggs out of the way. "Just move. I'll do it."

Just then, Jepson spotted something on the wall that made him smile. A framed photo of himself holding Berto.

Outside, the apes and human soldiers had managed to push back the robots near the swampy edge of the Rocket Garden. But the robots weren't giving up. They dug in and fired back.

"This is it, people… And, you know, apes." Hicks Called out. "The clamps are clear. You need to get going! Flight crew, get onboard, now! We'll hold them off." Johansen whistled to get the apes' attention and then repeated what the Lieutenant said in sign language. Most of them listened and peeled off to get in the rocket, but Bella wasn't having it. She was out front, firing away, pushing the robots back.

The rest of the astronauts climbed aboard while Captain Stack and Private Murray detached the fuel hose from the ship and let it drop to the ground. Jepson spotted Bella and called out to her. He signed that they had to go, but just, she kept on fighting.

Tears in his eyes, Jepson was about to give up and leave her behind. But then he saw it.

The bushes behind the robots seemed to explode! A massive alligator dove at the robot, grabbing it in her jaws. Then a second. And then a third, and several more. It must have been the whole nest, and boy, were they angry! Riding on top of the lead gators were Astro and snot, having the time of their lives!

Between the gunfire and the feeding frenzy, the robots couldn't keep up. Bella screamed at her brothers to quit playing around and get onboard. As they ran past her to the hatch, she made a point of smacking them each across the back of the head.

Just as they tried to slam the hatch closed, Giggs wriggled out, kicking free of the hands trying to pull him back in. He fell to the pavement, only to be grabbed by Stack. "Idiot. You'd have been better off going with them.... Whether or not they actually make it into space."

"That's it!" shouted the Lieutenant. "They're good to go! Everybody, fall back and take cover! It's about to get toasty!"

The soldiers kept firing as they backed off. Murray tried to pull the fuel hose away from the rocket. "Leave it!" Hicks told him. "Just go! Not into the machine shop! Get as many buildings between you and the engines as possible! Go, go, go!"

As the soldiers ducked around the corner of the building, they stopped firing and just ran. Past the visitor center, the gift shop, and the museum. That's when the rocket started up. Not with a boom, but a series of small clicks. Johansen looked to his captain and told him, "I expected more."

"What do I know? Maybe it just needs to warm up? It's been lying there for decades."

And then came the sound of a motor trying to kick over, winding, faster and faster.

The alligators must have heard it too, because that's when they let go of their prey and dove back into the swamp.

Click... KA-BOOOOM!!!! The engines fired, engulfing the entire Rocket Garden in flames. The force was astounding as the fire rebounded off the wall, pushing the Saturn V forward. Several robots were all but vaporized in the blast. Even more were destroyed when the fuel hose ignited and the machine shop exploded.

It was incredible... Though not at all pretty. The ship shot forward off the stand, its back-end setting fire to the trees as it passed too close above them. Out over the Atlantic Ocean, more than once, it skipped off the water, like a stone, looking like they would simply flip over and crash.

To say that tensions were high inside the ship would be more than a mild understatement. "Pull up! Pull up! Pull up!" Johnston yelled. "We're not supposed to be water skiing here!"

"Quit yelling at me!" Andreyev screamed back. "First ever horizontal launch of a three-hundred, fifty-foot rocket is not so easy!"

"We get it, Captain Obvious. Just do it!"

"If you don't shut up, I will turn this ship around!"

Titus was the first - but definitely not the last - to get sick. Kong, who hadn't buckled into his seat in time, was pressed against the back wall of the compartment from the G-force.

ROLLING THUNDER DRIVE-IN THEATRE

The bombers had made a huge crater in the center of the lot. The excavation robots moved in with the combat units, forming a perimeter. At the forefront was the drilling machine. It moved quickly through the now-softened earth. The robots were quick and efficient. As the drill churned up the ground, other machines cleared it away.

*****

Ford and his team had managed to get a safe distance below ground and avoid the blast, but now they needed to get back topside. The general was in great shape for a guy his age, but the stairway from bottom to top was taller than any skyscraper. He was out of breath.

"Sir," one of the Secret Service agents called out. "My men, two floors up say that the stairs gave way. There's a huge gap that we can't get past!"

"Of course, there is," Ford muttered. "We have to get back up there! I know what the robots on the ground were waiting for!" He racked his brain, looking around at the troops beside him. He shook his head when he remembered the apes behind him, and then he shouted to the agent. "Let the apes through!" And as they passed, he signed instructions.

"Did you just…" The agent asked him.

"Shut up. There'll be no living with her now."

"We're going to die here, Lindt!" Goodwin shouted. "Please tell me you've got something useful in your bag of tricks!"

"I've got a few bricks of C-4 that were meant to blow an entrance into that bunker and the EMP."

"That's it? I thought you were the demolitions expert?"

"Yeah, well, I thought your apes were here to keep the robots off our backs." He snapped.

"Fair enough," she answered. "Give me a second." Suddenly, she stood up and whistled as loud as she could. And believe me, it was LOUD!

Almost all of the apes heard the call and knew immediately who it came from. Like the angry and protective family that they were, they redoubled their efforts to save Dr. Goodwin. Suddenly looking like a swarm of bees, they pushed through.

Jackson spotted three baboons beating on a smaller robot made from Sogdo Motors. It was heavily armed, but still basically a car. "C'mon, Daniel. I have an idea." He, Daniel and Hercules fought their way across the field until they reached it. The baboons had the hood torn off and were trying to tear the motor out.

"I need that car!" Daniel signed frantically to the apes, who backed off. Then along with them, he laid down cover while his father checked the engine. It looked to still be working, but the door was locked and the window covered in metal.

"On it," Hercules grunted, in ape speak. It was fairly easy for him to simply rip the door off its hinges.

Jackson jumped in and ripped a few fuses out of the panel below the steering wheel. He crossed wires and the engine whirred to life. He put the car in gear, gripped the steering wheel, but then felt the whirring stop as the car stalled. "Sorry. It's been a while since I've gotten to drive. I'm out of practice." He re-started the engine and peeled out towards Goodwin and the soldiers.

"No way they'll all fit in that thing," Hercules pointed out to Daniel.

"Yeah," the boy agreed. "But he can clear a path to that bunker. We need to do what we can to help him!"

The great ape nodded, and with a deafening roar, charged after the car. The baboons and others let out a war cry in return and fought to give Jackson the room he needed to drive.

It didn't take long at all for the robots to figure out what was going on and refocus their attack on the car. Jackson was getting close, but maybe too late.

"What does he think he's doing?" Lindt wondered out loud.

"He's paving our way! Get ready to follow him!" the Doctor replied.

"Pull up! Pull up, pull up!" Jepson yelled. "We'll never escape the atmosphere at this angle!"

The rocket was picking up speed. It fought against the pull of gravity and trying to gain altitude. The apes were all squealing and screaming.

Andreyev answered through tightly gritted teeth, "Will you all please just shut up? This isn't like flying a plane. I can't just pull back on the controls! I know what I'm doing. I've been to space seven times!"

"Not like this, you haven't!"

"There's a first time for everything," Andreyev winked. "Johnston, stand by to release the first stage. Rodgers, when he does, I need you to fire all second stage boosters and thrusters!"

Johnston and Rodgers shared a skeptical, if not terrified glance. "Um, sir?" Johnston spoke up. "Isn't it too early to release the first stage? It's still almost a third full of fuel."

"I'm counting on it! This rocket was made to get to the moon. We're not going nearly that far. We let it loose and use the blast from the second stage to blow that tank. The concussion from the explosion should give us the additional thrust to break free. But you both have to fire at the exact same time."

"Wait, what?!" Jepson was incredulous. "Where did you learn science!? We'll be blown up along with it!"

"Maybe. If any of you has a better idea, now's the time. Otherwise, we fire in three…"

Jepson closed his eyes, Li took him by the hand. Johnston said, "…Two…", to which Rodgers responded, "One…"

All aboard, closed their eyes as the astronauts pressed their ignition buttons.

A.G.D.A. BUNKER

The apes formed a chain - one's hands holding the next one's ankles - and bridged the gap in the collapsed staircase.   One by one, the agents crawled across. Somewhere above them, the sound of drilling grew louder.

*****

Much deeper below in the War-Room, the dignitaries mostly stared at the ceiling. Some hid under tables, others huddled together while yelling at their aides to do something.

The chancellor of Germany and the president of the United States were pouring over paper schematics of the facility. "Who designed this place?" The German asked. "This is why I voted against building it in your country! There's no emergency exit?"

The American president pointed to the stairs. "That's it, right there. In case the elevator went out, we put in the stairs. Emergency lights and everything! What do expect, secret tunnels or something?"

"Yes! You idiot.   We're the government. Secret tunnels are what we do!"

"Well, I'm the American government. We use sewer tunnels."

"Wait. Sewer tunnels? Show me where."

*****

Even deeper below them, Grant was exhausted. His hands, bloody from digging. It was hot, and the air was thick with dust and debris making it hard to breathe. He was making no real progress getting through. He collapsed to his knees, with his head in his hands.

Something slapped him on the shoulder. "Ook ahh ooh ook."

Grant was stunned! He started signing a mile a minute. "Darwin? You're alright! You made it! How did you get through? Wait, no! How did you get back out?"

Darwin pointed to the open door. Duh! "I saw the sign that said 'exit'. You do remember that I can read, right? Did you hit your head or something?"

Grant jumped up and gave the ape a hug. Darwin patiently patted Grant on the back before pulling away. He signed, "So, are we doing this, or what?"

"Oh, yeah, I'm just glad you're not… Um, but you're right. We have work to do. C'mon." And they ran back into the circuit room.

SOUTHWEST SATELLITE ARRAY

The car plowed through the robots small enough to fit under the satellite dishes. Daniel clung to the hood, wildly firing the large automatic weapon mounted there. Two chimps with weapons of their own fired from the roof.

As they neared the trapped humans, Jackson skidded to a stop, nearly throwing the passengers atop and yelled, "Get behind us! C'mon, move, move, move!"

The soldiers fell in with Hercules and the apes behind the vehicle. Goodwin jumped into the passenger seat. "Nice ride. Thanks for the save."

"We're not saved yet. Buckle up". And Jackson gunned it towards the bunker.

SATURN V

Click-Ka-Boom!!! The first stage clamps released as the second stage fired all. The explosion threw the remaining part of the rocket into a wobble while nearly doubling their speed.

Andreyev fought to keep some semblance of control over the craft while the rest of the crew were pinned in their seats (Yes, even Kong) from the force. Li opened one eye and cautiously looked around. "We didn't explode? We made it! We…"

"Hold that thought! Brace yourselves!" Rodgers cut her off just as they hit the edge of the atmosphere.

The noise was deafening as the rocket jolted, shook wildly. The hull was starting to glow red from the heat. The seconds stretched out into what felt like hours as the ship seemed about to rattle itself to pieces.

And then, all at once, it stopped. I mean, not the rocket, of course. But it grew remarkably quiet and the turbulence disappeared. The second stage fuel tank went empty and Johnston hit the release. The module fell away gracefully.

"See? Easy, peasy. Welcome to space," Andreyev announced. He leaned over, gave Jepson a slug in the arm and told him, "I learned science from watching cartoons."

*****

Miles below them, the soldiers were casting off from the coast. Lieutenant Hicks and Captain Stack bumped fists as they watched the rocket leave the atmosphere, through binoculars.

Dr. Stanley Giggs said nothing as he sat, in the bottom of the raft with his hands zip tied behind him. Sgt. Johansen smacked him across the back of the head.

A.G.D.A BUNKER

General Ford was the last one across. As the agents continued onward up the stairs, he stayed back to make sure the apes all ended up safely on the right side of the chasm. When the last one was pulled up by her ankles, she held up a closed fist to the general. It took him a second before he understood and bumped it with his own.

What they didn't realize was that somewhere beside them, outside of the stairwell, the robots had actually drilled down past their current position. As a matter of fact, they were moments away from reaching the uppermost level of the bunker facility.

*****

The chancellor of Germany was flanked by security as she found the sewage tunnel. Her guards opened the hatch, and the smell was horrifying. She covered her nose and mouth with her handkerchief and used a flashlight to look in. "Oh, they're going to hate this. Alright, start bringing them in."

Leaders and representatives from nearly every country on the planet tend to be used to a certain amount of privilege. They're driven around in motorcades, live in stately homes, surrounded by the best foods, and are generally doted on. But now, every one of them was being shepherded into a dark, concrete sewer, ankle deep in grey water. It was really difficult for the chancellor to assure them that it was for their own good as she was fighting not to vomit.

*****

Down in the circuit room, Darwin and Grant were searching for the breakers. Darwin went to throw a switch, but Grant stopped him. "No." he said. "I thought you said you could read. We need the main switch."

The bunker was just ahead. Unfortunately, two huge robots stepped directly in front of it. These were among the more tactical robots that Jackson had seen. He turned to Goodwin and told her, "Jump! Now!" And when she realized what he meant to do, she opened the door and passed the message along to Daniel and the apes, riding outside. The boy leapt sideways onto Hercules' shoulders.

Once everyone had jumped clear, Jackson jammed his weapon down on the accelerator pedal, and jumped out himself. The car slammed into the leg of one of the robots at full speed. The massive machine lost balance and toppled, knocking into its partner before falling over and crushing the car. The vehicle's lithium battery exploded spectacularly, destroying the robots with it.

Lindt and his team rushed to take position behind the new, flaming barrier. The Captain attached his explosives to the solid metal doors of the bunker as the others laid down cover fire. The quarters were still too close for them to detonate.

The apes were fighting off the mechanical horde as best they could, but they continued to close in. Hercules handed Daniel off to Dr. Goodwin and went back to grab Jackson who was still on the ground covering his head.

The Silverback was too late. A robot with long spindly arms swooped in from nowhere, grabbing Jackson up. Its strafing gunfire forced Hercules to dive out of the way.

Daniel watched in horror as his father was stuffed into the robot's hollow torso. He tried to run to the rescue, but Goodwin swept an arm around him and pulled him behind the barrier.

"No!" He screamed. "Let me go! I have to save him!"

"Just get down and stay there. We're going to get your dad and I don't want to have to explain how I let you get killed!" She popped up and opened fire at the incoming enemy to clear a hole. Then she whistled again and pointed to the robot running off with Jackson inside.

"Herc! SMASH!!" she hollered.

And smash, he did! In a frenzy, the gorilla tackled the robot like a linebacker sacking the opposing quarterback. In football, Hercules would undoubtedly get flagged for unsportsmanlike conduct. His jaws clamped around the pistons in the mechanical neck, shaking back and forth until the head tore free. Meanwhile his powerful hands tore off the arms, all while keeping its legs pinned to the ground. Once the machine stopped moving, Hercules found the compartment seam and dug his fingers between, until he was able to grip and rip the body wide open.

Jackson was alive, but bloodied and half-conscious. Hercules picked him up and carried him, cradled in his arms like a child. Running was slower on two legs, but he managed to get to the barrier and lay Jackson at his son's feet.

Daniel grabbed his father and squeezed tightly as tears streamed down his cheeks. "Ow, ow, ow, ow!" Jackson moaned. "I'm alright. Just a little banged up".

Lindt's eyes went wide and he dove forward. But by the time anybody else had realized what was going on, the robot behind Hercules had fired four rounds. Bless him for trying, but there was no way the Captain could have shoved the massive gorilla out of the way. As a result, he simply ended up being a human shield… Mostly. One of the rounds tore through Hercules' upper arm. The other three caught Lindt squarely in the back.

The ape howled in pain and spun to defend himself, effectively flinging Captain Lindt sideways like a ragdoll. He lowered his head and charged, slamming the robot back and into the base of one of the satellite dishes. He grabbed its gun arm and turned it back on itself, blasting it to pieces. Then he tore off the arm and ran to attack the other robots with their own gun.

Lindt managed to sit up with a groan. "That is one tough ape."

"Tell me about it," Goodwin said. "And they just managed to make him angrier than I've ever seen. Seems like you're pretty tough, yourself."

"Luckily my pack caught the others. I'm fine," he answered as he pulled off the backpack and noticed wisps of smoke drifting from the new holes. He quickly unzipped the pack and pulled out the EMP with the slugs embedded in it. "I take back the 'luckily' part. This is bad."

"How bad?"

"Unless you plan to throw it like a brick, the EMP is useless. Best we can hope for is to retreat to camp and figure out plan-B."

"Absolutely not!" Goodwin commanded. "We retreat now, and there's no way we'll get back in later. I did not bring these apes all the way just to fumble the ball!"

"Can we still get inside the bunker?" Daniel asked. "There's got to be something in there we can use to shut it down."

"This isn't some light switch, kid. The Electro-Magnetic Pulse doesn't just turn it off, it essentially fries the circuits and permanently destroys any electronics within the perimeter. Without it, we can maybe shut down the satellite signal connection, but it wouldn't do anything to stop all these robots. We'd have to fight our way out again."

Jackson shook his head, "I can't believe I'm saying this but it's better than nothing. Disrupting the connection so they can't attack the rocket team was our primary mission anyway. Even if it's not permanent, it'll at least buy them some time to launch and get up to the space station. We have to try." He winked at Daniel who couldn't have been prouder.

Private Tapper interjected, "How do we even know the space team is still alive? We haven't heard anything from anyone."

"Then we don't know that they *didn't* make it." Goodwin responded. "So, until we hear differently, we stay on task, blow that bunker open and complete our mission."

SATURN V

The rocket drifted in space. On any prior mission, this was the moment that astronauts treasured. Quiet, floating in zero gravity with a spectacular view of Earth below. But this was nothing like any prior mission.

Bella floated through the capsule helping the other apes clean the insides of their helmets, trying to calm them and making sure they were properly strapped in. Dr. Li asked Jepson, "Are you alright?"

He considered the question a second. "I'd say I'll live, but we haven't even gotten to the fight yet." He hoped that it sounded like a joke, but the look on his face betrayed a lack of confidence.

Rodgers was going through a diagnostic checklist. Fuel level, battery life, etc. Johnston was doing the math, calculating their trajectory and time until contact with the space station. Andreyev was gingerly adjusting their angle and position.

"Sir, we've only got enough fuel for one shot at this, and we're basically eyeballing it in a ship that was built decades before the space station was even a consideration."

"What's your point?" Andreyev asked although he already knew.

"The station is travelling around the Earth at about seventeen-thousand miles-per-hour. If we miss, it'll take it approximately ninety-two minutes before it comes back around. Considering we'll be out of fuel and the station is being controlled by enemies..."

"So, you're saying, don't miss?" Andreyev interrupted. "That's all you needed to say. Don't miss."

Rodgers nodded. "I'm saying that if you miss, we float off into space and die."

"Got it, good note. Let's just hope your buddy Johnston's math is correct."

"Johnston interjected. "The station should pass here in six minutes, twenty-five seconds at thirteen degrees from our current position."

"Blah, blah, blah. Just tell me what I need to do."
Andreyev told him.

Johnston checked the gages and his notes.
"According to my usually impeccable math, you need to
adjust our angle by seven-point-five degrees and fire
thrusters in two minutes, forty-four seconds so we get ahead
of them and match the station's speed as it passes. Like you
said, easy, peasy."

"Assuming they don't try to shoot us down,"
Andreyev said.

"Isn't that what the satellite team was for, to keep
that from happening?"

"Again, assuming they made it. Alright, everybody.
Buckle up and get ready to puke… again."

The further the delegates went into the tunnel, the deeper the sewage got. For most of them it was now almost knee-deep. What's worse was that it was pitch dark. "Just keep moving," The German chancellor called out. This has to lead to a runoff, somewhere."

"Didn't the schematics show where it led?" the British Prime Minister asked.

"No. It just sort of ran off the edge of the page. But it's a sewer, there has to be an outlet."

"Americans…" the French delegate said. "We'll never find our way in this darkness. Does anybody have a lighter or matches, anything for some light?"

"NO!" shouted the German. "I repeat: Sewer! No telling what fumes are down here and we don't want to risk blowing ourselves up! Just use the walls to feel your way."

"Remember the days when we all would have had cell phones that we could have used? I'm not touching the walls, they're disgusting! I think I'd rather take my chances with the robots."

"You do realize what we're all wading through, don't you? It's a little late to be a germaphobe."

*****

Back in the circuit room, Grant announced, pointed to a big breaker switch. "This one! This is it,"

"Are you sure" Darwin signed.

"Hey, you're not the only one who can read". Grant answered with a grin. "Get ready, in three…"

Once more, crouched behind the counter of the concession stand, the general peeked out into what used to be the parking lot. Smoke and dust billowed up from the massive hole, surrounded by combat sentry units as dozens of smaller, man-sized robots scurried down. "Okay, I see four of them up top. Unknown how many are down below and how far they've gotten. What do we have from the armory?"

"Sir, we have two rocket launchers with two rounds, each. Small arms for each agent with about three magazines per. Four shotguns, fully loaded with seven rounds each and two bandoliers holding an additional twenty-one shells per."

Ford did the math in his head. "That's not a lot. Hopefully we can make enough noise up here so at least some of the others come back to check it out. Leave me the launchers. The apes and I will fight topside, you position your men, on each level below and protect those people."

"Then what, sir?"

"Then, I'm out of ideas. We'll have to wing it."

And that's exactly when the lights came on!

SOUTHWEST SATELLITE ARRAY

The explosion was massive. It Sent cinder blocks, huge metal doors and even the two fallen robots, in all directions. Shrapnel tore through nearby satellite dishes and robots alike.

Goodwin and her team took advantage of the few seconds of stunned confusion. They had taken refuge behind one dish, but had to run as it crumbled from the concussion.

Most of the apes were safe, as they were using the still standing dishes as high ground against the enemy. They too used the confusion to redouble their efforts. The tide was starting to turn and the apes were beginning to surround the robots in something of a crossfire.

Several ran towards the bunker and the doctor signed for them to take up position just outside as protection. "Hercules, you're in charge out here." The great ape threw her an exaggerated salute and laughed. In return she hugged him. "Try not to get hurt again." And with a wink she ran inside after her team.

Down the stairs they went. Slowly, in defensive formation. Passing the first level, which was mostly an office. On the second was barracks type living quarters. Third was a mess hall and kitchen.

It was the fourth level that they found what they wanted. This was the monitoring and server level. This was also where all the security was. Remote-controlled toy cars and Hobby quad-copters (Much tougher than they sound). All roaming the aisles, at the ready. As we know, robots are logical things.   And since bullets and explosives are generally not compatible with computer gear, they were armed with pneumatic dart guns.

The team was bottle-necked in the stairwell doorway. The lights were dim, other than the small LED's on the server terminals which Lindt estimated to be in the thousands. They stood in rows like library stacks. "We need to fall back and think this through. One of you men, hold this position. Do not engage unless provoked, but make sure nothing gets out."

The team retreated one floor up to the mess hall so they could use the tables to inventory their ammo.

"Can we shut them down?" Goodwin asked.

"It's possible, but I'm not liking the odds." Lindt told her. He had the EMP weapon's casing open and was sorting through its circuits, pulling out the three bullets.

"Options?" she pressed.

"Well," he thought. "Option one, we work our way through, shutting the servers down one by one. Which means going in there and fighting off the mini-bots in tight quarters. It could take hours and probable casualties to us."

"What about circuit breakers? Can't we just shut them down?"

"Same problem. In a government facility like this, they'd be on a dedicated circuit, which for security purposes, would be somewhere on the side of the level furthest from the entry."

"Sir," Tapper spoke up. "We have two grenades left. Why can't we just open that door and lob them in?"

"As a last resort, maybe. But we can't guarantee two grenades would destroy all the servers even if it brought this whole bunker down on top of us."

Jackson came out of the kitchen, and put a pot pie on the table where Daniel was resting his head in his hands. "You need to eat something, kid."

Everyone else just stopped and stared.

"What?" he asked.

"Where did you get that?" Lindt jumped up and pointed at the food.

"The freezer is full of them. It's no trouble, if you want...."

"You cooked it?"

"I'm sorry. Should I not have? I just thought that since they already knew we're here..."

"No. *How* did you cook it?"

"The microwave. Why?"

Lindt laughed out loud. "Of course! Jackson, you're a genius!"

Jackson shrugged, "It's no big deal, really. I put it in and pressed start."

But Lindt was already hurrying to the kitchen. He shouted back over his shoulder, "We can do this! …. Maybe. At least I think I we can do it!"

They all jumped up and followed him. He looked around and told them, "Okay, I need copper wiring. Everybody start pulling as much of it as you can from the other appliances."

"What are you going on about Lindt?" Goodwin demanded.

"What did people used to call it when they cooked in a microwave?" he asked in return. All she did was shrug.

"Nuking!" He answered for her. "They called it 'nuking the food!' Don't you see?"

"So, your plan is to use the microwave to what? Nuke the server room?"

Lindt was practically giddy. "No…. Well, yes. Sort of."

"Captain, are you sure you're fit for duty? You're not making any sense."

"I'm fine! Listen. Nuclear weapons release an Electro-Magnetic Pulse into the atmosphere when they detonate. Kind of like a solar flare. That's the same, or at least similar energy to how a microwave works. On a much smaller scale, obviously. Hence, 'nuking' your food! That's why I need the copper wiring. I may be able to fix the EMP, using the microwave! Get it?"

"Not even a little. But you're the demolitions expert and let's face it, it's probably no more absurd than anything else in this war."

"The upper level looked like an office. Take Jackson and see if they have any extension cords or power strips. The longer the better. Grab as many as you can find."

They went about their various assignments. The soldiers searched for copper wiring, Goodwin and Jackson headed back upstairs, Lindt started taking apart the microwave and Daniel? Well, he ate his pot pie. It would've just been stupid to waste it.

All in, it took roughly an hour to pull it together. There was no power outlet in the stairwell, so they had to daisy-chain the extension cords from the mess level. The EMP was suspended inside of the microwave, like a gyroscope, by the copper wiring. Two soldiers walked point as Lindt gingerly carried the device down the stairs.

The window was shattered and they found the soldier on the ground with a dart in his forehead. Tapper pressed two fingers to his neck. "He's alive, sir."

"Tranquilizers?" Goodwin asked. "Why?"

"Who knows?" Lindt shrugged. "Maybe they thought a prisoner would be useful? Information, maybe?"

Tapper checked inside the portal, and quickly ducked out of the way as a dart flew past and embedded in the ceiling. "Sir, I think they're waiting for us." And then they all had to get out of the way as a volley of about a dozen more darts whizzed past. Lindt, his two soldiers and Daniel dropped to the floor below the window frame and out of the line of fire. Jackson and Goodwin pressed themselves tightly against the walls. On the stairs, the last of the soldiers dropped to his knees and passed out with a dart in his arm.

"It's go-time, people. Tapper and Nelson, lay down suppressing fire, aim high and scatter the bots. On three."

"Wait!" Daniel called out. And then they all heard it. A twangy guitar supported by a snare drum rhythm with an ethereal voice singing.

"What? It's a radio." Jackson said. "Daniel, get out of there and let them do their jobs.

"No! It's a message. A signal." Daniel said. For us, from the general, it's got to be!"

"We don't have time for this!" Lindt reminded. "Why would you think that?"

Dr. Goodwin caught on. "The song. 'Star Crossed' by The Bitter Pills. The kid may be right. But why? They didn't even know you were here."

"I told Darwin, in case Dad didn't find my journal. It must mean the other team got through!"

"They could have sent that days ago. We have no way of knowing what they're trying to tell us." Tapper said.

"Look, one way or the other, we're here, now. Can we please just focus and get this done?"

Everyone nodded their consent and took position. The Captain tucked the weapon under his arm and silently counted down with his fingers.

The robots inside the server room scattered as the bullets flew. Lindt reached through the broken window to open the door from the inside. Keeping low, he pressed "1", "5" and "start" on the oven's key-pad and then slid it out as far into the server room as he could get it. "Go, go! Now!" he shouted as he bolted from the room, trying to pull the door shut behind him. He didn't make it. A dart stuck him in the neck, just behind his ear.

...13...

...12...

...11...

Tapper and Dr. Goodwin opened fire through the window as Nelson tried to drag the unconscious Captain out of the way but a dart caught him in the collar bone.

...9...

...8...

Jackson dove behind his son, taking a dart in the back. He slumped to the ground.

...7...

...6...

...5...

On the stairs, Dr. Goodwin kept firing as she backed away. Daniel saw her fall to a dart in the belly as he ran. Tapper never even made it to the stairs.

...4...

He felt the dart strike his calf and barely had time to react.

...2...

...1.

And as the world went dark, Daniel could still hear the song playing.

Barely alive, the standing crew of the station was locked in the cargo hold. Other than minimal food being slipped into the module, they had no contact with their captors. They were weak and movement had become difficult after being in zero-gravity for so long.

A red light on the bulkhead began to blink. It was the communications officer who first noticed it. He nudged his commanding officer who was sleeping, strapped in so he wouldn't drift off while he drifted off. "Something's happening, sir."

The Commander startled, and rubbed the sleep from his eyes. "Huh, what? What's happening?"

"I'm not sure. But the flashing light, it's a proximity alert, Sir."

"Have we changed orbital trajectory?"

"I wouldn't know, sir. I've been trapped in here with you. The light just started a few seconds ago."

Outside, the station's two mechanical arms whirred to life.

The parking lot was flooded with light. Sound was blasting from all the public address speakers. Each of the three movie projectors were running. It was chaos. One was playing an old western. A sheriff was running down a stagecoach robber on horseback.

The screen exploded as an ape swung through, mid-battle with a robot.

A pair of World War II aces were dogfighting high in the clouds on the second. A bomber flew through, dropping its payload over enemy lines. As the bombs hit their target, General Ford rolled away to avoid a robotic claw, trying to grab him.

One of the apes wasn't as lucky. Snatched up off the ground, he was thrown to yet another robot which stuffed him inside a steel compartment.

Two orangutans pushed with all their might, forcing one of the construction machines over the edge and down into the crater, which was now a half mile deep. The Machine belched out a ball of flame and oily smoke when it hit bottom, causing something of a hologram as it crossed the image from the third projector. A massive face claiming, "The end is near."

The general signed to a chimpanzee who nodded. Ford fired and ran into the path of a combat sentry. As it shifted to go after the old man, the chimp leapt from behind and skittered up its back. The robot went into a frenzy as its sensors registered the chimp tearing the hydraulics from its steel body. It fired its weapon wildly—almost desperately—at its unseen attacker, inadvertently blasting away its fellow sentry before toppling into the crater.

Ford rallied all the apes and told them to go after the last sentry. They attacked from all sides. Some smashed at its head with chunks of asphalt while tangling its legs with some downed telephone wire. When it fell, they all joined in dragging it towards the hole.

The general rushed over to stop them. He pointed at the large cylindrical torso and signed "Open it." The largest of the animals punched at a panel until it was bent enough to get his fingers under and then ripped it free.

Inside, their comrade was shaken up, but not too badly injured. Once the others helped him out, he looked to the general and saluted.

"Okay", Ford told them. "Now you can throw it in. With any luck it'll at least slow that drill down."

The robot crashed off the sides as it tumbled down the hole. The apes all beat their chests in triumph as they watched.

"We're not done yet. We have to get down there and help the others."

*****

Far below, the fortress shook with every explosion. The sound of drilling was nearly deafening as they hurried through the corridor. "We have to get back up there and help the others." Darwin told Grant.

"I just hope they're still up there to be helped. It's not looking or sounding promising."

Hercules was a born leader. His brothers and sisters loved, respected and probably even feared him a little. Since he didn't have Dr. Goodwin or Daniel to protect, he was able to let loose on the battlefield. He was at once graceful and brutal tearing through the enemy. And the others took their cues from him.

But the robots were relentless. They had no fear, no emotion, and they gave as good as they got. Better, in fact. The battle was again turning in their favor. Reinforcements had shown up and pushed back the apes, who were now just trying to survive.

The humans had been gone for too long now and Hercules feared the worst. Without Dr. Goodwin, it would be up to him to save his tribe.

And then the pulse hit.

It wasn't actually visible, but they all felt it. Almost like a burst of air.   The dishes all drooped to their lowest positions. Circuits fizzled, the robots faltered. Some took another step or two. Some just fell over. A few spun in drunken surges of energy before spitting out sparks.

The apes were confused. Several of them felt a wave of dizziness and nausea. Hercules didn't notice at first and just kept fighting. Other apes climbed down off of the now lifeless robots they had been battling.

The gunfire stopped. The battlefield had grown eerily quiet, and everything mechanical was simply dead.

They didn't puke. Well, most of them anyway. Titus had to tilt his chin up to keep from re-swallowing that which was sloshing around in his helmet. The entire crew were slammed back against their seats as the engines fired.

The few minutes at such velocity felt like forever. "You're going too fast! You'll overshoot the target path. Pull back on the thrusters!" Johnston said.

"I know what I'm doing." Andreyev answered. "Call out at one-minute, twenty-five seconds from contact. Jepson needs to prep the monkey and open the hatch. Make sure the cable gun is ready."

"That's the plan? Are you kidding me?" Rodgers panicked.

"Be like the apes. Don't overthink it."

"We're astronauts! Overthinking is in the job description! Who came up with this?"

"It was Dr. Giggs' idea, actually." Jepson chimed in.

"Of course, it was! Are you listening to yourselves? Wasn't Giggs the one working with the robots? I would rather it was the ape's idea!" Bella growled in response. "No offense." Rodgers quickly added. "Why don't we just let them fly the ship?!"

"Don't be ridiculous." Andreyev told him. "They were never good pilots."

"One-minute, twenty-five seconds out," Johnston reported.

"This is insane!"

"It's unpredictable. That's kind of the point." Jepson reminded him.

"One-minute, nineteen seconds to contact," Johnston continued.

"Copy that. Cutting thrusters… Now!" Andreyev announced.

Everything went quiet and the crew felt their guts return to their original positions as the force dissipated.

"Jepson, you're up. Li, help him with the hatch."

Dr. Jepson unbuckled himself and Kong then helped him put on a tiny extravehicular activity pack. Bella had undone her own restraint and hurried to the winch that was bolted to the cabin deck. She grabbed the clip on the cable's end and fastened it to Kong.

"Forty-five seconds to contact." Johnston called out.

"Li? Where are we with that hatch?" Andreyev asked as he struggled to hold the ship steady.

"Standing by, sir."

"Rodgers, how's our course?"

Stunned, Rodgers shrugged. "I.... Sir, at this point I just..."

"Not helpful, Rodgers. Next time maybe we let the apes navigate. Just help keep us steady."

"Yes sir."

"Thirty seconds to contact."

"Everybody check your helmet seals and oxygen levels." To which they each replied or signed, "Good check."

Jepson handed Kong the cable gun, which looked comically big in his little monkey hands.

Bella manned the winch, releasing the brake and unspooling the first several yards of line.

"Twenty seconds to contact."

"Enough, Johnston. We get it."

"Shutting up, sir."

Li opened the latches on the hatch. She made sure they were all ready before pushing it open.

With Kong on his shoulder, Jepson leaned out and searched the vast darkness outside. He spotted it after a moment. From here, it was little more than a glittering speck, but it looked to be catching up.

He plucked the monkey from his shoulder and nodded at Bella. Once she started the winch, Jepson said good luck to his little friend and threw him as far out as he could.

The station was now close enough that they could make out the structure in detail. The wide panels across the top, the tubular modules making up its fuselage, the robotic arms meant for holding and repairing satellites, and finally, the last shuttle to bring crew members up, still docked alongside.

"How's our course, Rodgers?" Andreyev asked.

Rodgers had resigned himself to just go with it. "Course is… good, I guess? Steady."

"Well, now steady yourself. You're going to hate this next part."

The apes were able to climb down the craggy walls of the crater. General Ford was lowering himself by a rope wrapped around his waist. He soon realized that it would be nowhere near long enough.

He called out to the apes, signed them all to stop and told a large orangutan that he was going to need a ride. Amidst the smoke and darkness, he made out movement. It was one of the excavation machines. But it looked lost, moving in random turns, spilling the rubble it collected down further into the hole like it didn't know what it was doing.

"Be ready to move fast," he signaled the others as he unshouldered the rocket launcher and took aim.

It was an easy shot, but the concussion from the explosion rattled everything. The apes clung tightly to the rock walls. As the robot fell, it bounced off the sides and smashed another robot in the process.

Ford climbed onto the orangutan's back and they continued their rapid descent. Far below them, they could now see what used to be the concrete roof of the bunker. The robots had made it inside.

*****

Grant and Darwin had made it to the War-Room where they stayed hidden and observed several of the smaller robots wandering aimlessly. They bumped into tables, walls and each other.

"Does this mean they did it?" Darwin asked.

Grant shrugged. "It looks that way. But that just means they're not connected to the main CPU anymore. They're still dangerous. We have to stay hidden until we can shut them down."

"And all the people? What happened to them?"

The rumbling above them had gotten extremely loud. The drill was only two levels above them.

"I have no idea. I was downstairs with you, remember? Hopefully they found a way out."

*****

The sewage pipe was now waist deep in sludge and water. The delegates had all given up on complaining and trudged onward using the slimy walls as guides.

Attached to the rocket only by the winch line, Kong righted himself using short bursts of air from the EVA pack. The station was getting close. The little capuchin took aim with the cable gun. It was noiseless when he fired. The cable unspooled, sending a small grapnel at the station.

The Saturn crew all waited with baited breath as the wire floated across space. The station was about to pass beside the rocket and they were all but sure the little monkey had missed. Until he didn't.

The grapnel hit the side of the station and dragged along the hull. It finally snagged on a hold bar for the astronauts on space walks. Kong gave it a tug to be sure it was secure, and then hit the retract button on the gun. He was pulled across the void until he could grab the same and then he unclipped the winch line from his belt and attached it to the space station.

"He's got it," Jepson shouted. The two craft were now anchored side by side, maybe twenty yards apart.

Bella started the winch, reeling in the line and pulling them closer to the station.

The station's arms flailed, trying to grab the Saturn rocket.

Astro and Snot didn't wait. They dove out the hatch and pulled themselves hand-over-hand, across the cable, to the station.

"You're right. I don't like this." Rodgers grumbled. The space station had now overtaken the rocket and was effectively dragging it.

"Did you not study the blueprints?" Andreyev asked him. "Where were you expecting to dock? How did you even get on this mission?"

"They didn't have anyone else." Rodgers reminded him.

Andreyev shrugged, "Gear up. We're going for a walk."

Johnston clipped a short cable, from his belt and to the winch line. Then he helped Jepson do the same.

"Remember, once you get across, unclip one end from your waist and attach it to the station's hull. Do not let yourself free float." Jepson nodded and followed Johnston out the hatch.

Titus was next. Li had to help him, as he was having trouble seeing through his splattered visor. She clipped herself on, and took his hand to guide him.

"Alright, Rodgers, you're next with Conan. You have to be fast. Once you clear the gap, make sure to release the winch line so we don't smash into the hull. We'll distract them while you and the others infiltrate the station. Then Bella and I will secure the ship and catch up with you."

"Copy that…. Wait, what? How?"

"We're going to get a helping hand. Now, move out."

Darwin shoved Grant back into the stairwell and slammed the door behind them, just in time.

The War-Room ceiling collapsed as the drilling robot broke through. Falling concrete smashed several of the wandering robots. Even with the remnants of the other robot on top of it, the drill kept onward towards the next level down.

"What do we do now?" Grant asked. In return, Darwin shrugged and pointed up the stairs. And as they went up, they didn't see the general and his team, repelling from the hole, in chase of the drill.

They jumped to the floor, clearing out the last of the smaller robots. "Anybody here?" Ford called out. There was no answer. He had no way of knowing that he'd missed his son by only seconds.

"What now?" the orangutan signed.

The general stooped and picked up the last remnants of charred schematics with a circle drawn around the sewage tunnel. "What else can we do? We stop that drill and hope the others found a way out." He reloaded the rocket launcher.

Several stories above, Grant and Darwin had to duck as the frightened Secret Service agents opened fire without realizing who they were shooting at.

"Hold your fire! We're on your side!" Grant screamed.

"Clear!" he heard one of the agents answer in return. "Come up slowly with your hands where we can see them."

They did as they were told, and once their identities were sufficiently proven, Grant asked, "Where are the others? The delegates."

"Unknown, sir. Because of the drilling, we haven't gotten any further into the complex than the stairs and haven't seen anyone. But if it's as ugly as it was up top, I wouldn't count on finding survivors."

"What about my father, I mean, General Ford?"

"He and the apes stayed topside to hold off the robots. But again, so many of them got in, I just assume they failed."

"Did you notice the robots were suddenly acting strange? Unfocused and random, like?"

"Sorry, sir. If you ask me, all robot behavior is strange. In the heat of battle, I didn't notice anything differ..."

BA-WHOOM!!! A massive explosion from the War-Room sent flames shooting up the stairwell like an exhaust pipe!

The agent pulled Grant and Darwin through a doorway, just as the fire would have incinerated them all.

The stairs crumbled and collapsed. They were trapped on what was left of the Behavioral Sciences level.

A.G.D.A. SPACE STATION

Johnston, Conan, Astro and Snot pulled themselves along the side of the hull towards the airlock. As soon as Rodgers was across, he unclipped the winch line.

The station's robotic arms swung and swiped wildly, trying to scrape them off the side. Titus attacked the base of one, punching and pulling with all his might to no avail. He instead just looked like a cowboy riding a mechanical bull.

Li and Jepson clung tightly to the base of the wide solar panels while Kong tried to pull the grate off an exhaust vent.

The Saturn V drifted away from the station with the winch cable streaming like a kite tail. Bella stood, waiting just inside the doorway.

Andreyev used short thruster bursts to maneuver the command module. He rotated its position, under the station and towards the arms. "Bella!" he called out and then signed to her, "Get ready. This is going to be rough."

The free arm snapped its large claw, trying to grab the capsule. It clanged off the side, shoving it out of position. "Ahh, ooh eek!" Bella screamed.

"I know, I know. If you think you can do better then you come drive!" the astronaut replied as he fought to course correct.

Titus finally got hold of the other arm's hydraulic line. His face slammed into the puke splattered visor, reminding the chimp that he was wearing a helmet and couldn't bite through it. It took all his strength to pull it free. Fluid and sparks spit out and the arm went limp, which only seemed to anger the station. Alarms wailed and red lights flashed. The other arm lashed out for the Saturn V.

Rodgers guided Jepson and Li to join the others where Johnston and Conan almost had the hatch open. "Well, they definitely know we're here now."

Andreyev swung the Saturn around and knocked into the second arm. The whole station lurched and Snot lost his grip. Conan yelped as Astro grabbed his tail, using it to swing out and catch his brother before he could float away.

"Sorry!" Andreyev called out. "My bad!" And then muttered to himself, "C'mon, stupid robot. I'm right here." And moved in for a second try. The arm narrowly missed again.

The outer airlock was open. Johnston ushered the others inside. As he brought up the rear, Rodgers asked, "What is that maniac trying to do?"

"We'll give him two minutes before I close the outer hatch and resume the mission."

The third try did the trick. The mechanical claw clamped tightly around the rocket and pulled it in close. "That's it! Gotcha!" Andreyev cheered. "Bella, Go! Now, do it now!"

Using the winch cable, Bella swung out. She quickly wound the line around and around the arm, tightly constricting its joints so it could no longer move and then around the capsule, essentially tying it in place so the claw couldn't let go.

Once it was as secure as it could be, Andreyev unbuckled and climbed onto the station. He and Bella hurried to the airlock, pulled it shut and sealed it behind them.

"What were you doing out there? We were about to go on without you two." Rodgers spoke up.

"What can I tell you? The parking sucks here."

Bella signed, "Where's Kong?" That was the first anybody had noticed he was missing.

The agents stood guard over the hole through the level as well as the stairwell. Grant was typing away at a computer terminal. "I don't know how much it helped in the fight, but at least now we can use the security feeds to track the robots and search for survivors." He frantically began clicking through the facility's cameras. Darwin took a seat at the next terminal over and did the same.

Two of the cameras up at the theatre were nothing but static. A third showed a dirty, cracked lens lying on its side on the ground. It was hard to make out anything other than flames and smashed metal. Finally, a camera atop the concession stand gave them an idea of the topside situation. It looked like total destruction, but at least they couldn't see any more robots moving in.

Level by level, they scrolled through the feeds. Above their current position, the obstacle course level and apes living quarters both showed the same thing; A huge central crater, a few small fires and random robots wandering aimlessly in the same confused manner.

Next, was the level they currently occupied. Same central crater, and other than seeing themselves on one camera, it looked clear.

They moved on to the War-Room feed. It was decimated. All the furniture and the monitor wall were smashed and charred. The fires seemed to be out. At least the suppression systems were still working. The drilling robot looked to have made it partially through to the following level when something blew it up.

"Geez! We were just down there and couldn't find anybody on the level. That must have been the explosion that took out the stairs. I still don't see any bodies, but I also don't think anybody could've survived that blast.

Darwin smacked Grant on the arm. "There!" he pointed. On the N.S.E.P. training level, something was moving in the giant pool. Again, it was hard to see clearly through the smoke and steam. The pool water was murky from all the debris and ash, but there was definitely movement. Darwin zoomed in as best he could.

Everyone in the room let out a gasp and then a cheer when they saw him. It was General Ford!

He was dragging the injured orangutan over to the side of the pool where the other apes helped to lift them both out of the water. "Go!" Grant ordered the agents. "Find ropes or whatever you need, but get down there and help them now!"

<u>SPACE STATION</u>

With the outer door closed, Johnston opened the inner hatch to the station. Li checked the readout mounted into the wall and confirmed life support.

"We have to keep moving." Jepson told Bella. "The station knows it's under attack, and we have to finish before it finds a way to fight back or upload itself to another source. We have no idea what we're facing here, so keep sharp and keep on task. This is what we signed on for."

The alarm suddenly quieted. It was replaced by a deep mechanical voice that sounded like a malevolent smart phone assistant. "You didn't think it would be that easy, did you? You will report immediately to the cargo module."

From the far end of the corridor, two small robots - seemingly built from lab gear - emerged.

"I wouldn't call what we did so far 'easy'." Andreyev answered.

"Failure to comply will result in termination of you and the crew of this station."

"They're still alive? After all this time?" Li asked out loud. The computer didn't answer. "That explains why the life support system is still operational."

"But why would it keep them alive?" Rodgers asked.

"We can ask them when we see them." Andreyev said.

"You're not really suggesting that we go willingly, are you?" Jepson demanded.

"You have a better idea, Doctor? There are eight people alive up here who know much more than we do. We can see what sort of condition they're in, why they haven't fought back, and if there are defenses that we are unaware of."

"The station will expect us to try something and likely be ready." Johnson interjected."

"Exactly. So, our best option is to behave counter to that."

"You have ten seconds to comply." And the robots closed in. There was barely room for the team to move, let alone fight in the weightless environment.

"We're going, we're going. Don't get your nuts in a bolt." Rodgers said as he put up his hands.

But Titus had other ideas. He threw open his visor, shaking his head violently. The vile smelling, chunky liquid spewed out into the zero-gravity, splattering everywhere… And everyone!

The humans all recoiled in horror, but Conan saw his chance. He dove at the robots. Even the shock from a small electric prod it held couldn't stop him. Astro and Snot thought it was hilarious and sprang into action!

"I guess that's that." Jepson said. "Seems they had a better idea after all."

"Quick, Li, get to the cargo hold, and get the crew into their helmets! Johnson, make sure all external communications are cut off. Rodgers, you get to their shuttle and make sure Omni can't keep it from taking off."

Bella looked to Andreyev, awaiting her orders. "What?" he signed. "Go help your brothers break stuff!"

"Initiating life support system shutdown," the computer warned.

"Hurry up everyone, the crew will have maybe half-an-hour of oxygen once the life support system shuts down!"

*****

Kong was trapped in the exhaust duct. The alarms were extremely loud. Between the flashing red lights and his helmet fogging up, it was hard to see. When the station got hit and the sirens went off, a panel slid into place and blocked the open vent. He had no choice but to find out where the duct led. It wasn't easy even for a monkey as small as him to turn around in the tight space. Once he did he began to shimmy his way inward.

The apes opened fire at the massive hole in the ceiling. The agents screamed at them to hold their fire, but it was too late. One of the ropes snapped and an agent fell the nearly thirty feet into the water below.

General Ford simply held up a closed fist and the shots immediately stopped. "Whoa, whoa, that's enough!" he said. And then to the agents, "They don't speak English, remember?"

"Yeah, but we can't sign and hold onto the ropes at the same time!" said the agent as he swam towards the edge of the pool.

"Fair enough. 'Bout time you joined the fight." He offered a hand, helping the agent up.

"It looks like you and your team did pretty well without us, sir."

"What about the delegates? Did you get them out?"

"Negative, sir. They're just gone. No idea where, but we ran into Grant and one of the apes. They turned everything back on and are safe up in Behavioral Testing."

By now the other agents had touched down and gathered around.

"I noticed. And not a moment too soon. Glad to hear they're safe." The general gave it some thought. "I think I have a pretty good idea where the others went. Come with us."

SOUTHWEST SATELLITE ARRAY

Daniel felt as if he was floating on air as he blinked against the blinding light in his eyes. Nothing made sense. For like the millionth time in his life, he wondered why he wasn't dead. Or was he? The last thing he remembered was trying to run up the stairs. He didn't know how, but he knew he was moving. There was something soft, like a carpet, rubbing against his face. He shook his head, trying to clear his vision.

The first thing he could make out was the sky. The next was Hercules smiling down at him. He was cradling the boy in the crook of his arm, carrying him. They were crossing the battlefield where most of the apes were checking to make sure the robots were really destroyed.

"Where's Dad, Dr. Goodwin and the others?" he asked. Luckily, he could sign it because his mouth was completely dry and it would hurt to speak.

"Others took them back to camp." Hercules answered. "They were sleeping, like you"

By the time they finally got back to the old ranch, Daniel felt like he could walk again. Jackson ran up with a big jug of water and handed it to the boy. "Thank God you're alright! I really thought we were done for that time."

"Nah," came Dr. Goodwin. "I never doubted for a second." Captain Lindt was beside her. "Turns out, that kid of yours is nothing but good luck."

"So, we did it? We shut them down. Does that mean we won?" Daniel asked.

"I couldn't say." She answered. "We shut down the satellite dishes and all the robots in the area. As far we know, they don't have their global hive mind anymore. Which should at least confuse them or make them drop their programming, but we don't know about anyone else. We tried sending a message to the bunker, but nobody's answering. We have no way of contacting the space team. If they don't complete their mission and destroy the central computer, we're back to square one. All we can do is hope."

It was actually pretty impressive what Omni was able to make little robots out of on the space station. Bella escorted Jepson and Li to the hold, smashing at little mechanical arms, prods and a lunar rover as they went.

"Sir," Johnston said. "External coms are down."

"You're sure it can't get them back up?" Andreyev confirmed.

Johnston tossed him a circuit board with frayed wires coming off it. "Pretty sure, Sir."

"Good. Go help Rodgers with that shuttle. We need it if we're going to get everybody off this thing." Astro and Snot led Andreyev towards the command module. Omni tried to slam shut each hatch they reached. But each time, one of the apes would move faster and wedge it open.

"Life support system shutdown complete. Internal atmospheric purge in one minute," the computer announced.

"That's not good. Go help the others!" Andreyev told the apes as he continued trying to hack the central computer.

On screen it said, "System lock out. Unauthorized entry. Switching to alternate encryption."

He spotted a fire extinguisher and pulled it from the wall. "You didn't think it would be that easy, did you? Encrypt this!" And he started smashing the computer.

"Internal atmospheric purge in forty-five seconds." And then another of the small prods extended from the panel and delivered Andreyev a shock, strong enough to throw him across the compartment.

Kong came to the end of the duct and found himself in the avionics compartment. All that meant to him was that there were lots and lots of wires and circuit boards. He grinned.

The crew of the station could hear the ruckus outside the compartment, though they were in little condition to do anything about it. They pressed their backs against the far wall as the hatch hissed open.

"Suit up, now!" Li shouted at them. She and Jepson started helping them as quickly as possible.

The four apes got to the cargo bay. It was small and crowded. "Help them to their ship!" Jepson told them. And as the crewmembers suited up, the apes took them.

"Thanks, I can manage," the commanding officer said and pushed himself off along the walls.

One of the others chimed in, "So, are we not going to talk about the fact that we're being rescued by monkeys, or am I hallucinating?"

"We can discuss that on the flight home. For now, just move" Jepson told him.

"Internal atmospheric purge, thirty seconds."

As they reached the shuttle, Jepson said to the two astronauts, "Please tell me this thing will still fly!"

"Buckle up, we'll find out." Rodgers said.

Concerned, Bella looked around and then suddenly bolted back through the airlock. Everyone was stunned. "What is she doing?" Johnson asked. "Wait, where's Andreyev?"

Bella threw herself through the station until she found Andreyev unconscious on the floor. She grabbed him by the head and shook him until his eyes opened.

Over the helmet com, Johnston called out, "Sir, we have to seal the shuttle airlock before the station purges. If we don't, it'll suck the air out of here too and we'll be crushed like an empty can!"

He looked at Bella, and signed "I'm sorry." And then to Johnston. "Don't wait for us. We're not going to make it." And he was glad she couldn't understand his spoken words although he suspected she knew what was going on.

There was a long silence from the shuttle until, "Yes, sir. It's been an honor, sir. God speed to you both." And contact broke off.

Bella and Andreyev watched through a portal as outside, the shuttle's thrusters fired and it separated from the station.

"Internal atmospheric purge, ten seconds.

She threw an arm around his shoulder and lifted him up. "What are you doing?" he asked her. She simply rolled her eyes and dragged him over to the hatch they first arrived through. She clipped her line to a bar and opened the hatch.

Just then, Kong burst from a small door in the ceiling and jumped into Bella's arms.

"Internal atmospheric purge, commencing."

Pfft…. And that was it. No implosion, no heroic death.

She signed to Andreyev, "Humans are so dramatic. Open door, relieve pressure. No big deal."

"Right. I knew that." Andreyev chuckled.

Kong squealed and hissed as he signed for the human's benefit. "We go home now.

"Not yet, we don't. We have to shut down that system first."

"Oh, I bypassed the power regulator. The station is going to blow any minute." Kong informed them.

"You did what, now?" the Russian asked.

And then the alarms started again.

Andreyev jumped up and went to the monitor. The screen said, "System failure. Overload warning."

"Wait," he asked. "How did you…?"

"What? I know science. Darwin taught me. Don't over think it."

"Right. We should go now."

SPACE SHUTTLE

It was a spectacular explosion. The concussion rocked the shuttle as Johnston fought to keep it lined up for re-entry into the atmosphere. The whole crew knew what that meant and bowed their heads in silence.

Moments later, Rodgers tried the radio. "Command, this is station flight crew. Come in. Repeat, this is station flight crew, do you copy?" and then they waited for a reply.

"Flight crew, this is command. We copy." Ford said into the radio. They were crowded into the behavioral testing level. The smell was awful as the delegates were still covered in filth from the sewer. "It's good to hear your voice. Can we get a situation report?"

The old radio crackled. After a moment, "Mission accomplished, sir. Omni is destroyed, personnel recovered."

The cheer of the crowd was deafening. High fives, hugs… quick ones, nobody wanted to touch each other. "Great job, flight crew. We'll have cold drinks and warm beds waiting for you when you return. We've got you on radar and you're clear for landing at N.S.E.P. Fly safe."

"Yes, sir. Thank you, sir." But there was little enthusiasm in his voice.

The Florida coast was visible out the window. Johnston pulled back on the controls, lifting the shuttle's nose to slow themselves. "Speed and angle, looking good. Trajectory is spot on. ETA…? What the…? Rodgers, are you seeing this?"

"I've got a blip on screen, but it's not in our course. Debris from the station?"

"Negative. Any debris that size would have burned up. Forget the radar. Look out there!" And he pointed off to the North-East, over the ocean.

"Huh… Well what do you know about that?"

The bottom glowed from the heat of re-entry. Three parachutes bloomed from the top. The capsule splashed down safely in the water even before the shuttle touched on the tarmac.

An away raft sped across the water from the waiting military catamaran. The capsule's hatch blew open. No sooner did the raft pull up beside it when Kong sprung out.

Captain Stack hooked the handle with a pole and leaned into the hatch. "Really," he said. "You let the ape drive?" Bella grinned and clapped her hands from the pilot seat.

"After everything we've been through? What did I have to lose?"

Andreyev and Bella climbed aboard and headed in to meet the shuttle team.

<u>ALL ACROSS THE GLOBE</u>

Survivors were emerging from their hiding places. For the first time in a long time, they were unafraid to go outdoors.

Word had gone out by telegraph. Government leaders took to the streets themselves to spread the word. People were rediscovering things that they hadn't seen in years. Some were being introduced to things they'd never experienced before and only heard stories about.

Memorials were held for those lost. Celebrations for those able to reconnect. People had become so used to fending for themselves and having to put in the hard work to survive, maybe that wasn't such a bad thing.

The Sogdo Motor company demolished their factory to great public fanfare.

It would still be a long time before the planet went back to normal. Or better yet, humankind had learned its lesson and would instead do things differently.

Do things better.

ROLLING THUNDER DRIVE-IN THEATRE

Two months after the final battle against the robots, the wrecked movie theatre seemed an appropriate place for them all to meet. It was a happy reunion, though a little bittersweet.

Dr. Jessica Goodwin-Ford looked around and her heart swelled. She was surrounded by her amazing extended family. All together for the first time with no other reason than they wanted to be.

Grant and Darwin had become inseparable. Rumor had it they were working together on interstellar space travel.

The once again retired general was manning the grill. When Stanley Jepson told him that he would burn the sausages if he didn't flip them, Ford smacked him across the back of the head. The two of them laughed and raised a toast.

And of course, there were the apes. Bella and Hercules never got enough of one-upping each other with their war stories. She never let him forget that she actually went into space, and he was very proud of the scar on his arm. But without fail, Kong would remind them both that it was he who actually destroyed the master robot.

Astro and Snot barely remembered the war. They just wanted to play.

Daniel loved this new world. He loved all the people and especially the apes who stood by him, protected him and taught him. But something was missing. A hole in his heart he didn't know would ever be filled. He sat in the newly grown grass that was reclaiming the drive-in lot, just watching everyone around him.

Jackson knew something was still bothering his son. He was proud of the man Daniel was becoming and had learned to trust his instincts completely. It was time for the world to move forward and Jackson would help however he could so that Daniel could move on with it. He went and sat beside his son. "You okay?"

Daniel nodded. "Just thinking." he said. "It still doesn't make sense. All those people the robots took. Why? In New Mexico, why did they tranquilize us instead of killing us? What were they doing with them, and could there still be a chance that they're alive? Maybe even just some of them? I just don't feel like this is over until we find them, or at least find out what happened to them."

Jackson understood what he was really talking about. "Look around you. You were such a huge part of what we did here. You helped win the war, Kiddo. I'd be willing to bet you a new Mp3 player that there's people who would be willing to help you get those answers.

Stanley Giggs sat with his hands cuffed tightly to a table. Only a single dim lightbulb overhead. Blank concrete walls surrounded him. He looked tired, worn and frail.

The heavy iron door swung open and Hercules filled its frame. He grunted.

"Really? It'll be a little hard to have a conversation since I can't very well sign with my hands like this." He chuckled.

The silverback growled and took a sharp hop into the room, startling the doctor. From behind him stepped first Bella and then Daniel. Bella took up position next to Hercules while Daniel sat in a chair across from Giggs.

"So, this is what it's come to?" The doctor. smirked. "They sent a little boy and his pets to protect him? I did what I had to, to survive. I won't apologize for it."

Now it was Daniel who smirked. "I know a thing or two about survival, too. You don't do it by selling out your planet. You do it with the ones you care about. The ones who would gladly fight or die by your side and you'd do the same for them. These two aren't my pets, they're my family. And you've got it backwards. They're not here to protect me from you. They're here to protect you from me."

This time, Giggs laughed out loud. "What an adorable child. Why don't you go tell the grown-ups that I'll tell them everything I know when they're willing to come make a deal to release me."

But Daniel didn't budge. "You really don't get it. There's no deal. All those people the robots took. That's on you. You knew what they were doing and you helped them. You made your deal with the robots. How'd that work out for you?"

Giggs made a show of yawning. "Look, little boy. As precious as you are, I'm tired. So, for the sake of saving time, how about you just tell me what it is you want?"

Daniel stood, he leaned in close to the doctor. "I want what all little boys want. I want my mother!"